BEST FRIEND NEXT DOOR

BEST
FRIEND
NEXT
DOOR

Carolyn Mackler

Scholastic Inc.

ISBN 978-0-545-70945-3

10 9 8 7 6 5 4 3 2 1   17 18 19 20 21

Printed in the U.S.A.   40
First printing 2017

Book design by Abby Kuperstock

To my son Miles, whose name scrumbles to spell smile *(perfect)* *and* limes *(yum) and* miels *(the plural of* honey *in French).*

〜〜〜〜〜〜〜〜〜〜

one

HANNAH

My name is Hannah Strafel. Hannah is a palindrome, which means it's the same backward and forward. Strafel spelled backward is Lefarts, which sounds French. As in *Le Farts*. Unless the French have another word for fart, which they probably do. I've never looked that up.

If I were going to look up any word in French right now, it would be *terrible*. Right now, my life is terrible in every single language. For one, my best friend, Sophie, just moved to Ottawa. That's a city in Canada, almost three hundred miles from western New York. I'm sure she's making tons of new friends there and will soon forget I exist. Sophie and I lived next door to each other on Centennial Avenue since we were toddlers. I can't imagine life without her.

Reason two that things are terrible: Sophie's house wasn't empty six hours when a real estate agent teetered across the lawn in her spiky heels and hooked a SOLD!!! pendant under the FOR SALE sign. I bet she SOLD!!! it to old people who hate kids. Or murderers. Or worse, a family full of girls who will take over Sophie's room at the top of the stairs and paint her walls pink and have slumber parties on Sophie's floor, where we used to roll out *our* sleeping bags.

"Hannah?" my stepmom, Margo, calls from the kitchen. "Are you almost done?"

I'm sitting on the side porch. I was supposed to be shucking a bowl of corn, but I've been watching a man move boxes into Sophie's house instead. Another man is wheeling furniture up the driveway on a cart. They arrived a little while ago. At first I thought they were the new neighbors until I saw that their van said MOVING ASSOCIATES.

"Are you almost finished with the corn?" Margo says. "Dad just got home from the store and we want to talk with you."

"Coming," I say. Even though I've only shucked three ears, I've strewn corn silk all over the porch. I brush it into the trash bag that Margo gave me. "I'm not done, though."

"Bring it inside!" my dad calls from the kitchen. "We can help."

I stand up, holding the heavy bowl in my arms. Margo must have put twenty ears of corn in here. I'm strong, though. I've been on the Dolphins swim team since third grade. Freestyle is my best stroke. Everyone says I have muscular arms. That's the plus side. The downside is that my short sandy hair is greenish from the past month of swim camp. Margo says she's getting me a new shampoo because my Ultra Swim shampoo isn't working.

"Hey, Hannah," my dad says. He unclips his bike helmet and washes his hands at the sink.

Margo is at the table, slicing tomatoes. There are hot dogs and veggie burgers defrosting on the counter. We're having a barbecue in our backyard tonight. Uncle Peter is coming over and a few of my dad's friends and some people Margo knows from her book group. If Sophie still lived here, her family would be invited, but she's probably having a barbecue with her new friends in Canada.

And then there's reason number three: Fifth grade starts in two weeks. I went online this morning and found out I have Mr. Bryce. I've never had a guy teacher before. I bet he's the strictest teacher at Greeley Elementary. I bet he yells if you're late and only lets you drink water once a day.

"I got you a peanut butter cookie at Crumbles," my dad says, taking the corn from me and setting it on the table. He gestures to a small white paper bag. "Just save it until after lunch, okay?"

Peanut butter is my all-time, hands-down favorite food. Even so, my heart races with suspicion. Something about how my parents are both grinning makes me think they're going to tell me awful news. I'm being a worrier, but that's the way I am. It's *who* I am. Just like how I swim competitively and my birthday is on New Year's Day and I'm the only kid in Greeley who hates pizza.

Sure enough, my dad grabs an ear of corn, tugs off the husk, and says, "There's something big that we want to share with you."

"We're going to be telling people tonight," Margo adds, shifting her smile to my dad, "but we wanted you to know first."

Hang on! Maybe they're going to tell me that we're moving, too. Please let it be Canada. I've always liked the maple-leaf flag. I will learn to love massive amounts of snow. I will get over my fear of ice-skating.

"The thing is," my dad says, "we're having a baby."

My stomach flips over. Actually, it's more like a triple somersault. Margo reaches across the table and touches my hand.

I yank my fingers away. "I thought you didn't want more kids."

Margo is forty-two and my dad is forty-seven. Not like it's any of my business, but isn't that too old to be having a *baby*? Also, she and my dad are always saying how, now that I'm older, we can start traveling and doing cool things. Not to mention that Margo is in the process of adopting me. Margo has been my stepmom since I was one. Before that, it was just my dad and me. I never even knew my real mother. They've already done all the paperwork for the adoption and talked to lawyers. After the adoption goes through, our true family was going to be the three of us. Not the FOUR of us.

"Honey," Margo says gently, "we were hoping you'd be excited."

"Can you believe you're going to be a sister?" my dad asks.

"No," I snap. I've been an only child for almost eleven years. "Please don't call me a sister. I'll be a former only child."

My dad laughs. He doesn't get that I'm not kidding.

"You'll get used to it," he says. "You'll have plenty of time to adjust by February."

February? That's only six months away. I happen to know it takes nine months for a baby to come out. That means they haven't been telling me the truth for three whole months.

Margo tips her head to one side. "I'm a little more than three months pregnant, if that's what you're wondering. We wanted to make sure everything was okay before we told you."

"We didn't want you to worry," my dad adds.

This can't be happening.

"What about the Bahamas?" I ask. My dad, Margo, and I have been talking about going to a tropical island this winter. Supposedly it's a swimmer's paradise because the ocean is crystal clear. It was going to be the biggest deal of my life. Every school break we either stay in Greeley or go to Pennsylvania to visit Margo's parents. All of last year, we were watching plane ticket prices. I suddenly realize they didn't mention the tropical trip all summer. I should have suspected something.

"The Bahamas can't happen this February," my dad says, reaching over to tousle my hair. "Don't worry, Hannah. We'll make it up to you."

I dodge my dad. There are a million things I want to say,

like *maybe you could have consulted with me before ruining my life?* Or *how could you drop this baby bomb so soon after Sophie left?* Instead I mutter, "I am *not* okay with this." Then I grab my cookie off the counter and shove through the door.

As soon as I reach the porch, I look across our side yard at Sophie's house and smudge the tears from my eyes. If Sophie were still here, I'd run next door, go up to her room, flop onto her bed, and have a serious cry. Because I know what's really going on. I've been a fine stand-in kid for my dad and Margo, but now they want a real child of their own.

A silver car slows in front of Sophie's house. The blinker is flashing. As the car steers into her driveway, I notice it's towing a U-Haul trailer. Not a good sign. I clench the cookie bag in my hand and hold my breath.

A tall woman emerges from the driver's side and stretches her arms over her head. A shorter woman with blond hair and big sunglasses opens the passenger door. *So far, so good.* But then the back door opens and a smallish girl steps out. She's barefoot and really tan, especially her arms. Her hair is short and sandy, almost exactly like mine. And the weirdest thing is that she's wearing the same blue tie-dye tank top that I am. Margo got it for me at Old Navy last week.

As the two women walk toward the front door, the girl stands there looking around. It's almost like she's searching for something, except the street is deserted. The only sound is a baby down the block wailing. *Ugh.* I don't want to think about babies.

"Hey," the girl says. "I guess you're the girl that the real estate agent told my moms about. You're thirty-seven Centennial Avenue, right?"

I bite at my thumbnail. I hadn't realized she could see me up here on the porch. I hadn't realized that high-heeled real estate agent was using *me* to sell Sophie's house. If I'd known that, I wouldn't have helped Sophie make her bed and straighten her room before every showing.

"Hey," I say. For some reason, I start down our steps. I totally shouldn't. I should leave it at *hey* and go back into my house. But I'm sure my dad and Margo will pounce on me and want to talk about my *feelings* about having a baby the moment I go inside.

In other words, I'm stuck.

"We just moved here," the girl says, coming across the driveway and into my side yard.

As she gets closer, I can see that she has a constellation of freckles across her nose and her toenails are all painted different shades of blue.

"Nice shirt, by the way," she says to me.

I wish I'd worn my yellow T-shirt. Or the green striped one. Anything but the exact same blue tie-dye tank top.

"What's your name?" the girl asks.

"Hannah," I say.

She laughs and shakes her head. I stare her down like *Okay . . . what's the big joke?* Sophie used to say I have a killer stare when I'm mad.

"Sorry, it's just funny because my name is Emme, with an 'e' at the end. We're both palindromes. That means it's spelled—"

"I know what a palindrome is," I snap.

Emme shrugs. "What grade are you going into?"

"Fifth," I say. From her size, I'm guessing she's going into fourth or maybe even third. "Greeley Elementary. I'm ten."

"Me too!" she says. "At least I think that's the name of the school."

I squeeze the paper bag tight in my hand and feel the peanut butter cookie inside breaking into pieces. There are four different fifth-grade classes at Greeley Elementary, which means there's a good chance Emme won't be in mine. But she probably will be, with the way things are going.

"Do you know who your teacher is yet?" I ask.

Emme shakes her head. "This all happened fast. We just found out a few weeks ago that we were moving for sure. Actually, *I* just found out. They'd been planning it for a while."

She says it like she wants me to feel sorry for her. Well, I don't. She can't just move into my best friend's house and expect me to welcome her with a hug.

"Everyone thinks I'm younger," Emme says, "but I turn eleven on New Year's Day."

"No way." This can't be happening. "No. Way."

"What?"

"That's my birthday, too," I say quietly. "New Year's Day."

"For real?"

I nod. This is all getting a little weird.

Emme starts giggling. "Mom J!" she shouts. "Mom C! You won't believe it! The girl next door has my birthday!"

Her birthday?

As the two women come out of the house, it dawns on me: Emme has two moms and I don't even have one to call my own. I feel an angry itch inside at the unevenness—the *unfairness*—of this.

"I'm Julia," the short blond woman says, waving at me. "It's nice to meet you. You two have the same shirt on! And you're a New Year's baby? Do you know what time you were born?"

I shake my head.

"Not exactly *baby*," Emme says.

"I'm Claire," says the tall woman. "I'm so glad Emme's already made a friend next door."

Not exactly *friend*! I glance at Emme. Her cheeks are flushed and she's staring at her feet. For a second, I feel bad for her the way her mom said we're friends.

As soon as the moms head back into the house, I blurt out, "Do you like peanut butter?" I know that's random, but I'm hoping to find a few more ways that Emme's different from me. Ideally, she will be allergic to nuts. Not bad allergic, like Marley from school, who has to carry an EpiPen wherever she goes. But just allergic enough to leave me with my peanut butter obsession.

"That's so funny," Emme says, grinning. "I love peanut butter *anything*. Almost as much as I hate—"

I cut her off. "Pizza?"

She opens her eyes big. "How did you know that I hate pizza?"

No! She cannot love peanut butter AND hate pizza. Without saying anything, I turn and storm into my house.

I don't want a baby in my life, and I definitely don't want an identical twin.

two

~~~~~~~~~~~~~~~~~~

EMME

I still can't believe we've left Florida and moved to Greeley, New York. For the first ten (and three-quarters) years of my life, I lived on Captiva Island with my moms and my fat orange cat. We had the ocean on one side and the bay on the other. Now we live in a small town where the only body of water is the YMCA pool. I used to collect shells on the beach and swim outside every day and set up my easel and sketch tropical flowers on our back porch. Now I'm sitting in an empty bedroom at the top of the stairs, staring at the paint samples that Mom J brought me this morning. She selected shades of pink like Luscious Blush, Diva, and Sunrise Surprise. I haven't liked pink since kindergarten. I'm more of a periwinkle blue kind of girl.

For the four days that we've been here, Mom J (otherwise

known as Julia, or my short mom) has been pointing out all the "great" things about Greeley. She says we'll go to an apple orchard this fall and plant a garden in the spring and go strawberry picking next summer. Like that's supposed to make me happy about moving. Fruit is fine and all, but it's not like a fresh peach can hang out with me and help me decide what I'm going to wear for the first day of school.

"Lunch is ready, Em," Mom C calls up the stairs. That's Claire (or my tall mom). Up until now, Mom C has been the stay-at-home parent. But starting tomorrow my moms are trading places. Mom C will be working at a big law firm in Rochester. That's why we moved here. "Peanut-butter-and-banana sandwiches. Crusts cut off."

"And local apples!" Mom J chimes in.

As if a local apple a day can keep the loneliness away.

"Emme!" Mom C calls again. "No ignoring. We know you're up there."

My cat, Butterball, is curled in a mound outside my door. I heave him into my arms and head down the stairs. He immediately starts purring. He loves being cradled like a baby. We think it's because he was a stray when he was little, so he's making up for his lost kittenhood. Back in Captiva, my friends and I used to dress him in bonnets and bibs.

When I get to the kitchen, Mom C and Mom J are laughing. They've been a couple since college. People always comment on how perfect they are together. I guess it's true, but recently they've been annoying me. Maybe it was the long drive up north. Or maybe it was how they didn't give me a choice about leaving Captiva Island.

"What amazing apples," Mom C says as we sit on stools at the kitchen counter. Mom J sliced them onto a plate, with a sprinkle of cinnamon and nutmeg.

Mom J passes the apples to me. "If it doesn't rain, let's check out an orchard when Mom C goes to work tomorrow."

"Do you really think picking apples will make me feel better about leaving Captiva?" I grumble, looking around the kitchen. A lot of our stuff is still in cardboard boxes stacked against one wall. We haven't even hung any photos yet. "I don't think I'm going to make it here through the fall."

"Are you starting the *Back in Captiva* thing again?" Mom C asks. "I thought you said you'd *try* to like Greeley."

I lick a glob of peanut butter off the side of my sandwich.

"Yeah, where's my glass-half-full daughter?" Mom J says. She's always talking about how we're both optimists.

"Your glass-half-full daughter is back in Captiva," I say.

They laugh like it's a joke, but I'm not finding it funny. I know the truth is that I have to survive fall and winter and spring (and every season until . . . forever). It was a big deal when Mom C got hired as a lawyer at this firm. Mom J quit her job at the newspaper. She's going to stay home and write during the day and drive me wherever I need to go. I'm going to try out for swim team and find a place to ice-skate, just like I did in Florida. People don't realize there are rinks in Florida, but it's true.

"What about Butterball?" Mom J asks.

"That's right," Mom C says, nodding brightly. "That's a definite plus about being here."

It's true that my cat's life has improved in Greeley. Back in Captiva, we lived in an apartment on the second floor of a house. Butterball's only fresh-air time was on the screened porch, where he'd pace the perimeter, meowing angrily. Here in Greeley, we have a backyard with trees to scratch and birds to stalk. Anytime Butterball wants to go outside, he squeezes his round body through the cat door and romps around Centennial Avenue.

I sigh heavily. "I guess so."

"Did you look over those paint samples?" Mom J asks. "Once we get your room decorated, you'll feel much more settled in."

"What about seeing if the girl next door wants to hang out?" Mom C suggests. "Hannah, right? She seemed nice."

I set down my sandwich. I don't want to tell my moms that their paint choices are hideous. Or that the girl next door hated me the instant she met me. It's not my fault we have the same birthday and I was wearing my tie-dye shirt! I decide not to respond because then they'll start in on how I'm being glass-half-empty.

Honestly, at the moment, it's hard to find a drip of *anything* in the glass. The glass is bone-dry.

~~~~~

The next morning, it's raining hard out. Mom C comes into my room early to give me a kiss good-bye. I rub my eyes. It's weird to see her dressed in a charcoal-colored suit, her hair blown straight. I'm used to the stay-at-home Mom C— ponytail, jeans, T-shirts.

When I get downstairs, Mom J makes me yogurt and toast, jots a few things on the grocery list, then disappears down the hall with a crate of papers in her arms. Back in Captiva (here I go again), Mom J used to cover parenting issues for the local paper. Now she's going to write articles for magazines. I've told her that, since I'm almost eleven,

I'm not sure I want her writing about me. When I was little, she'd publish articles like "Potty-Training Emme and Other Disasters." At least my classmates couldn't read at that point or I would have been the laughingstock of preschool.

"Want to see a movie this afternoon?" Mom J calls from her office. She's clunking around in there, setting things up. "It looks like it's going to rain all day."

I bet it's sunny on Captiva Island. School has already started down there, but I bet my friends Olivia and Lucy are going to the beach later this afternoon.

"Okay," I say, spreading jam on my toast. I wish Hannah seemed nicer because it would be fun having a friend right next door. I doubt that's going to happen, though, especially with the way she slammed her door on me that first day. I've spotted her on her side porch a few times since then, but we haven't talked.

I take a bite of toast, swirl around my yogurt with my spoon, and watch the raindrops sliding down the window. I guess I'll work on my shell drawings. On the drive up from Captiva, I drew pictures of shells from my collecting bag. My plan is to arrange the sketches on a piece of tagboard and glue real shells around the border. I'm going to send it to my cousin, Leesa, at her dorm. She's in tenth grade at a boarding school in Connecticut and she's artistic like me. Ever since last year, we've been mailing pieces of tagboard back and forth and adding on to each other's until we have a complete collage. We're already on our third back-and-forth collage.

As I carry my bowl to the sink, I glance at the food in Butterball's dish. The rule in our family is that whoever gets up first has to fork in a (disgusting) can of Oceanfish and Tuna. Otherwise, Butterball will wail and nip at our ankles. The vet says we need to get him to lose weight, but it'll never happen with the way he bugs us for his meals.

Butterball usually gulps down his food in eight seconds, but today he hasn't touched it. I try to remember the last time I saw him. When I was falling asleep last night, he was stretched around my head on the pillow.

"Mom J!" I shout, hurrying into her office. I'm not supposed to interrupt her when she's writing, but this is feeling like an emergency situation.

"Did you feed Butterball this morning?" I ask. "Or did Mom C? Because his food is still in his dish."

Mom J shakes her head. "I fed him around six thirty when I was making coffee." She turns back to her computer. "Come to think of it, he wasn't there. I just put the food in and assumed he was still in your room."

"Well, he wasn't!"

"Did you look in the backyard?" Mom J asks. "Try shaking the cat treats."

We still haven't unpacked my raincoat, but I hurry into the mudroom to put on my boots. Back in Captiva (okay, that's my last one), we definitely didn't have a mudroom.

Outside, the rain is still coming down. There are bloated pink worms writhing on the gravel path. I stand in the yard, rattling a container of Friskies Party Mix and calling, "Butterball! Here, kitty, kitty, kitty! *Butterbaaaaall!*"

But no Butterball. I wait at least ten minutes. By the time I come back inside, I'm drenched.

I'm kicking off my boots when I remember that yesterday, as I was brushing Butterball, I took off his collar. It's a yellow collar with a bell and two tags. One tag is from the vet in Florida and the other has Mom C's phone number. I dash into the living room, hoping one of my moms buckled his collar back on last night. But there it is, curled on the floor by Butterball's scratching post.

I burst back into Mom J's office. I feel a sob choking my throat. "Butterball didn't come when I called and I took off his collar yesterday and now, if he's lost, no one will know how to contact us."

"He's probably just exploring the neighborhood," Mom J says. "Put on some dry clothes. You're soaking wet."

"So is Butterball, wherever he is." I lean against Mom J's desk and start crying. One thing about me is that I cry easily. I can't help it. The tears come and there's nothing I can do to stop them. "If he's gone it's all my fault."

Mom J pushes out of her chair and wraps me in a hug. "He'll come back, Em. But how about we go to an early movie and then get lunch out? That'll keep your mind off things."

"No pizza," I say, wiping my eyes. Pizza grosses me out. If I'm even at the same *table* as someone eating pizza, I have to look away. Nobody believes me when I say that, which is why it was so weird that the girl next door specifically *asked* if I hated pizza.

"Of course not," Mom J says. "Never pizza."

After I change, we drive to the mall. They have a six-screen theater connected to an arcade. I generally love movies, but I can barely concentrate. I tap my feet all through the show and keep asking Mom J if she thinks Butterball will be there when we get home.

"Hopefully," Mom J whispers. "Let's think on the bright side."

I nod weakly. The problem is, I just said good-bye to my friends and Captiva Island. I can't handle losing my cat as well.

When the movie is over, Mom J squeezes my hand. "Maybe we'll have lunch at home instead. That way we can check for Butterball."

But when we walk into the kitchen, Butterball's food is still in his dish. It's dry and crusty and starting to reek. As Mom J scrapes it into the trash, my eyes prickle with tears.

"Did you tell Mom C?" I ask.

Mom J nods. "I texted her before."

"What did she say?"

"She said he's probably out exploring."

But when Mom C gets home from work, it's still raining and Butterball is still missing. Mom J makes my favorite dinner, spicy peanut noodles. I can barely eat it. Mom C and I go outside and call for Butterball. No luck. I try to read but I can't get through a page. I go outside and call for Butterball for another ten minutes. This time I get soaking wet and my moms make me take a shower even though I'm totally not in the mood.

Mom J comes in to kiss me good night. "He'll come back," she says.

I clutch Butterball's bib under my pillow and wipe back tears. "Did you know that *doom* spelled backward is *mood*? That's what I'm in right now. A *doom mood*. That's a palindrome."

"Uh-huh," Mom J says, yawning. "Why don't you try getting some sleep? It's been a long day."

All night I hear the rain against my window. I try not to picture Butterball wet and scared and alone in this brand-new town.

<p style="text-align:center">~~~~~</p>

As soon as I wake up, I check the whole house for Butterball. Nothing. At least the rain has stopped. I wonder if he attempted to walk back to Captiva. I've read about heroic cats who follow their families for thousands of miles. But Butterball is so fat I can't imagine him waddling even one mile.

Even his empty litter box makes me sad. Okay, that's gross.

I peek into Mom J's office. "Can you help me make missing posters for Butterball?"

"Sure," she says. "Mom C drove around looking for him before work, and I just checked the neighborhood, too. Making posters is another great idea."

We spend the next few minutes designing a sign on the computer. It says:

MISSING

Large orange cat named "Butterball."
Purrs when you hold him in your arms.

Beneath Mom J's phone number, we insert a picture of me holding Butterball. It's back in Captiva, and we're in the beanbag chair on our porch.

Mom J prints out fifteen copies and I grab a roll of packing tape. I can see out the window that the sidewalks are muddy. I slide into my Crocs and we walk around the neighborhood, putting up signs on poles and lampposts.

When we get home, I keep checking Mom J's phone to see if anyone has called or texted. Nothing yet. But I feel better knowing we did something to help find Butterball.

My feet got dirty while we were out, so I go upstairs and soak them in the tub. Then I get nail polish remover and a cotton ball and wipe the chipped shades of blue off my toes. I always have multicolored toenails. Today I'm going to paint them burgundy and silver, alternating toes, because I've heard those are the Greeley Elementary School colors. No one can say I'm not trying.

A half hour later, my newly polished toenails are dry. I'm just coming down to the kitchen for juice when I hear a meow at the cat door.

"Butterball!" I squeal, scrambling across the room and lifting him up. "Mom J! He's home!"

Mom J rushes in and we dance around the kitchen. I can't believe it. Butterball is home. Or at least as home as we can be in Greeley.

I bury my face in his thick fur, but then jerk back in surprise.

Butterball is wearing a new blue collar around his neck.

"We knew he'd come home," Mom J says, grinning. "See, it all worked out!"

I smile at her. For some reason I decide not to show her the blue collar. As soon as she leaves to take down the MISSING signs, I remove the new collar and fasten on Butterball's regular yellow one. Then I shove the blue collar behind the cat food, far out of sight.

Two days later, Mom J and I are walking to the farmers' market. Greeley has one every Thursday and Sunday. Mom J has been talking about it all morning. You'd think she's never eaten fresh vegetables before. I keep that thought to myself, though. Ever since Butterball returned home, I'm trying to be an optimist again.

We're right in front of the post office when I freeze. "Look!" I say.

"What?" Mom J asks.

I point to the nearest lamppost, where a sign says:

MISSING
Large orange cat. Answers to the name "Radar."
Likes to be scratched under the neck.
We only had him for a few days, but he's a sweetie.
We miss him like crazy.

On the bottom is a phone number and a photo of that girl next door. *Hannah!* In her lap, she's holding a fat orange cat.

"That's not *Radar*," I say. "It's Butterball! He was with the girl next door. She must have put that collar on him."

"What collar?" Mom J asks.

I flush. Now it seems silly that I didn't tell her. "Nothing . . . it's just that Butterball came home with a new blue collar on. I took it off."

Mom J grins. "That must have been where he went. Old Butterball. He didn't make it very far."

Mom J pulls her phone out of her tote bag and taps the screen. While it's ringing, she hands it to me.

"Hello?" a woman's voice asks.

"I'm calling about the cat in the sign," I say. "Umm, Radar?"

"Oh!" the woman chirps. "I'm Margo. Let me grab my daughter, Hannah. She's the one who found him. She's been so upset since he took off."

As I wait, I stare at the picture of Hannah smiling as she cuddles Butterball. When I met her the other day, she seemed pretty unfriendly. Maybe I got it wrong, though.

After a moment, Hannah comes on. "Hello?"

"Hi, this is Emme Hoffman-Shields." I pause. "I'm the one who just moved in next door, with the same birth—"

"I know who you are," she says.

Or maybe I got it right after all.

I clear my throat. "I saw your sign about my cat."

"*Your* cat?"

"Yeah," I say. I pause and glance at Mom J. "The cat isn't a stray. He's my cat. He ran away for a couple days and now he's home."

"Oh," Hannah says.

"Yeah. I just wanted to tell you that."

After a second, Hannah says, "Okay, well . . . thanks."

"Yeah, sure," I say. "Bye."

I hang up and hand the phone to Mom J.

"What'd she say?" Mom J asks.

"Not much. I mean, Butterball is *my* cat. What can she say?"

"So it *was* Hannah who had him?"

I nod. "She doesn't seem very nice."

Mom J links arms with me and we cross the street to the farmers' market. "Maybe she's going through a hard time," she says after a minute.

I have to admit the farmers' market is cool. Two men are playing banjo and there are free samples everywhere. Mom J buys turnips (ugh) and chard (okay) and beets (double ugh) and piles them into her tote. She gets me a peach (healthy) and an apple-cider donut (crusted in sugar) for a snack. I go for the donut first.

As we're walking home again, I start thinking about Hannah. Even though she only had Butterball for a short time, maybe she feels as bad as I felt when he ran away.

"Mom J?" I ask, wiping my fingers on my shorts. "Do you still have that girl Hannah's number?"

"Sure."

"Can I call her again?"

Mom J hands me her phone. This time, when the woman answers, I say, "Is Hannah there?"

"May I tell her who's calling?" Hannah's mom asks. I think she said her name was Margo.

"It's Emme again . . . with the cat."

When Hannah comes on, I quickly say, "His name is Butterball, but you can call him Radar if you want. It's a palindrome, after all."

Hannah doesn't say anything, so I continue talking.

"And we already have the same birthday and the same shirt, so if you want to share my cat . . ." I pause. "That's okay with me."

"Are you serious?" Hannah asks. Her voice is practically a whisper. "You'd share Radar with me?"

"Butterball," I say. "Or Radarball. Whatever. You can

come and pet him anytime, and he can even sleep at your house now and then. I mean, we're right next door."

I glance at Mom J. She's walking a little ahead, swinging her tote bag.

"I actually have some things that my stepmom bought for him," Hannah says. "A catnip mouse and a string toy. Catnip makes him crazy."

"I know!" I say, giggling. Hang on, did Hannah say *stepmom*? I suddenly want to ask her a million questions. Like how come she has a stepmom? Are her parents divorced? And who lived in my house before we moved in? And does she like swimming? And who's her fifth-grade teacher? Mom J and I went by the school yesterday to drop off forms and found out I have Ms. Linhart.

We turn onto Centennial. I see Hannah's house and my house in the distance.

"I know this sounds strange," I say, "but I'm obsessed with palindromes. Whenever I hear a new one, I—"

"Am I loco, Lima?" Hannah asks, cutting me off.

"Yes!" I shriek so loudly that Mom J turns around and raises one eyebrow. I wave my hand like *It's cool*, and she keeps walking. "Or *Ma has a ham*."

"Oh, great palindrome," Hannah says, "even though I hate ham."

"Me too!" I scream. This time, Mom J raises both eyebrows.

Hannah giggles. "Why am I not surprised?"

Maybe I'm being an optimist, but I can't help blurting out, "Hannah? It feels like we *have* to become friends."

At that exact second, Hannah opens her front door and steps onto her porch. She puts down the phone and waves at me. I wave back at her.

It's almost like she knew I was coming.

three

HANNAH

Okay, I'll admit it. Things are getting a little better. School started and it's not terrible. I might even like it. Fifth grade means we get to walk to the cafeteria and recess by ourselves. And I like volleyball in gym. It's fun to bump the ball over the net and I'm getting good at serving. Everyone says it helps that I'm tall.

It's a sunny Saturday morning. On Saturdays my dad usually cooks hash browns. But all this week Margo has been complaining that onions make her want to puke. She says it's *morning* sickness except it lasts *all day long*. And it's not just onions. She runs from the kitchen, covering her mouth if she smells broccoli or—*yep*—peanut butter.

Which is only my favorite thing on the planet. I'm trying not to take that personally.

My dad makes multigrain waffles for breakfast instead. As we sit at the table I don't join their conversation about how whole grains are good for a growing baby. Snore.

I clear my plate and head up to my room. My dad, Margo, and I have a big, scary, possibly exciting appointment this afternoon. The appointment is so big and scary and possibly exciting that I can't think about it or *I'll* throw up just like Margo. And so, to get my mind off the two hours and seventeen minutes until we leave for the appointment, I grab a sheet of paper and sit at my desk.

I draw a dark gray line down the center of the paper. On one side I write *Things that are good*. On the other side of the line, I write *Things that stink*.

I look out my window. I can see Emme in her backyard with her tall mom, Claire. Claire is the one who is a lawyer and goes to work every day. Sophie's family hardly ever used the backyard but Emme and her moms are out there all the time. They're always weeding the garden or reading in lawn chairs. Sometimes I go over and hang out with them. Ever since I found Emme's cat, things have gotten better between us. One time Emme's other mom, Julia, made us pear slices with peanut butter and we ate them on a picnic blanket in her yard. Another time we helped Julia hang a wooden glider on the swing set. It's cool that Emme and I are becoming friends. I feel bad that I wasn't very nice to her when she moved in, but she caught me at the worst possible moment.

Under *Things that are good*, I write:

Meeting Emme

After Emme's name, I add:

Liking school

I was so nervous about having a guy teacher, but Mr. Bryce has turned out to be The Best. He's funny and nice and he wears silly ties, like one with smiley faces or another with golden retrievers. Emme isn't in my class—she has Ms. Linhart—but I have girls like Layla and Marley and Natalie, who are all nice.

I move my pencil to the next line and write:

Swim team starting next Tuesday

The Dolphins, a youth team through the YMCA, practice twice during the week and also on Saturday mornings. Coach Missy says I'm going to rock the fifty freestyle this year.

I glance at *Things that stink* and chew on my pencil.

Missing Sophie, I write.

I *do* miss Sophie, but it's not as bad as I thought it would be. When I'm at school or hanging out with Emme I don't think about the fact that she lives in Canada now. That's when

I start feeling guilty and vow to send her a real letter. I promised I would write to her when we talked last week. I've started a few letters, but for some reason I can't get past *Dear Sophie.*

Not having peanut butter in the kitchen until Margo gets over her morning sickness, I add to the list of things that stink.

That, of course, brings me to the stinkiest of the stinks.

My dad and Margo having a you-know-what

I can't even write the *B*-word.

I crumple up my paper and throw it into the trash can. Then I worry that someone will see it in the trash and read it. So I fish it out, tear the paper into tiny pieces, and sprinkle it like snowflakes back into the garbage.

"Hannah?" Margo calls upstairs. "I was just talking to Emme and her moms in their backyard. Emme asked if you want to come over and hang out."

"Right now?" I ask. "Do I have time?"

"Just be home by eleven thirty to change into something nice and have lunch."

My stomach flips over. Everyone who knows me knows that I live in jeans and shorts and sweatpants. I don't even own a skirt. "Change?" I ask. "Am I supposed to get dressed up for this appointment?"

"It might be nice." Margo pauses. I can hear her talking with my dad. "No, it's okay. Wear whatever makes you comfortable."

"The appointment is going to be easy, Hannah," my dad says. "Nothing to worry about."

Yeah, right.

~~~~~

Here's the thing about Emme: She asks a ton of questions. She says that she inherited the interviewing trait from Julia, who is a journalist. And since Claire is a lawyer, Emme was basically born to cross-examine.

"What do you think?" Emme asks, holding up two strips of light blue paint samples. "I mean, what color do you like the most? Which one makes you think, *This is a real bedroom*?"

We're sprawled on the floor of Sophie's old room. Butterball—yep, I've stopped thinking of him as Radar—is curled in my lap, purring happily. It's the first time I've been up here since Sophie left. Emme's got a bed with a stuffed rabbit on the pillow, a white dresser, and all these containers of art supplies. It's strange to think this isn't Sophie's

room anymore, especially since I can see the little green smiley face that Sophie once scribbled on the wall next to the
closet door.

"What is it?" Emme asks, turning her head. "Are you
looking at the smiley face on the wall?"

I nod. "Sophie drew it a long time ago. She was happy
about something. I think the tooth fairy."

"I was wondering about that," Emme says. Then she turns
back to me. "It's probably weird to be here. Does it make you
miss her?"

I pat Butterball's soft belly. "It's okay."

"I miss my friends in Captiva. Sometimes I wonder what
they think when they walk by my old house. We used to live
two blocks from the beach."

"That's so cool," I say.

I stretch across Emme's rug. I've never met anyone before
who lived on a tropical island. And I love the way Emme calls
her moms *Mom C* and *Mom J*. She told me it used to be *Mama*
and *Mommy*, but when that started sounding babyish she
switched to *Mom C* and *Mom J*. It's awesome that she got to
pick what she calls her parents.

"So what do you think?" Emme slides the paint samples

toward me. "Blue Allure or Gulf Stream? Those are my top choices."

"Blue Allure," I say. "It sounds mysterious."

Emme nods. "Agreed."

"I'm just glad you're not painting the room pink."

Emme pounds the floor with her hand. She does it so loudly that Butterball jumps off my lap and waddles from the room. "I can't stand pink! Why does everyone think girls should like pink? It's so annoying."

"Agreed," I say. "Completely."

"I have an idea," Emme says as she circles *Blue Allure* with a pen. "I'm going to take a survey of you and we'll figure out everything we have in common. Are you ready?"

I stare curiously at Emme. This is totally not something Sophie would have done. Sophie was into watching reruns of *America's Next Top Model* and trying on her mom's makeup.

"You really want to interview me?" I ask.

"What else can we do? I can't have any more screen time. My moms have cut off my iPad for the rest of the day."

"How much time do you usually get?"

"Thirty minutes on weekends." Emme sticks out her bottom lip like she's pouting. "Basically nothing."

"Me too!"

"Why am I not surprised?" Emme flops onto her elbows. "Okay, let's get started. Your favorite color is also blue, right?"

"Blue Allure," I say, giggling.

"And we're both only children," Emme says.

"Yep." I stare down at my hands. It's not like I have a brother or sister yet. I'm totally an only child. Completely.

"I know your favorite food is peanut butter," Emme says. "Where were you born?"

I pause. I don't really talk about that. My past, at least the first few months of my life, is kind of weird.

"Colorado," I say quickly, hoping she doesn't ask anything else about it.

"Darn. For me it was Florida. But isn't it funny that we were born on the exact same day? What about art? Do you draw or paint?"

I glance at the sketches on Emme's wall. If she did them herself, then she's really talented. "No artistic abilities other than the time I made a double fishtail bracelet at day camp. What about you?"

"I love art. At least we're different in a few ways. What's your favorite palindrome?"

I pause to think. "I guess it would be *Did Hannah see bees? Hannah did.*"

"I love that one!" Emme says, grinning. "You can do it with *Emme*, too."

"What about you?"

"I made one up when Butterball was missing. Or should we call him Radarball?"

I laugh. "*Butterball* is fine."

"The one I made up was *doom mood*."

I shake my head. "I was totally in a doom mood this morning."

"Why?" Emme asks. Of course she does.

Just as I'm trying to figure out how NOT to explain my complicated life, Claire shouts upstairs, "Hannah! Your dad just called into the backyard. They need you at home. Something about an appointment?"

I hop up quickly. "I better go."

"Go, dog," Emme says, walking me to her bedroom door.

I stare at her for a second before I burst out laughing.

"Palindrome!" we both shout at the same time.

~~~~~

"Are you ready?" my dad asks, turning in the seat to look at me.

Margo is driving and my dad is in the passenger seat.

My dad isn't the typical dad who loves cars. He usually rides his bike everywhere, even to his office in downtown Greeley.

"I'm okay," I say quietly. I chew on my thumbnail but then quickly pull it out of my mouth. It took all of third grade to quit that habit.

"Ryan just wants to meet you and say hi," my dad says. "That's it."

Ryan is the lawyer they've hired to help Margo adopt me. Mostly they're keeping me out of the legal stuff, but now that we're getting closer to the adoption being finalized the lawyer wants to see if I have any questions.

"We'll be in the appointment with you the whole time," Margo says. "Ryan was nice enough to see us on a Saturday so we wouldn't miss work and you wouldn't miss school."

"And think about this," my dad says. "We'll be one step closer to the adoption being official. All our paperwork is in order. The court date could even be this fall."

I swallow hard and stare out the window. I'm not trying to be sulky. It's just that, in moments like these, words leak out of my brain. I bet Emme doesn't have that issue. She always seems to have something to say.

"Tell you what," Margo says. "How about we swing by the house after the meeting and get our suits and go to the pool? The Y has family swim this afternoon."

"Can Emme come?" I ask. "That might be fun."

Margo nods and hands her phone to my dad. "Can you call Julia for me?" she asks. "The number is in my contacts."

For some reason that makes me nervous. Like if Margo and Julia are talking on the phone, then maybe my stepmom is going to tell her about being pregnant. That would be terrible because I haven't told Emme yet. I haven't told Sophie, either, or anyone at school.

"Why do you have Emme's mom's number?" I ask.

"From when they called about Radar," Margo says.

"Butterball," I say.

"Hi," my dad is saying into the phone. "This is Drew, Hannah's dad. We wanted to see if we could take Emme to the pool this afternoon. The one at the YMCA?"

My dad turns to me. "Emme is shrieking in the background."

"What's she saying?" I ask.

"That's wonderful," my dad says to Emme's mom. "How long was Emme on the swim team in Florida?"

"No way!" I shout. "She swims like me?"

"Yep," my dad says, holding up a finger to me like *hang on*. "Emme is asking something. What's that, Julia? She's asking her mom to ask you if the pool is Blue Allure. Do you have any idea what that means?"

"Tell her yes," I say, smiling. "Tell her the pool is totally Blue Allure."

four

EMME

That's my spot," Gina whispers to me as I'm sitting on the meeting rug with my notebook in my lap, waiting for the math lesson to start. "In case you haven't figured that out."

I jump a little. I hadn't even seen her coming. I have the worst fifth-grade class ever (especially Gina, Alexa, and Haley). Even Ms. Linhart. It's an all-around disaster.

"Yeah, Emme," Alexa says, smirking at me. She has bright red hair and her two front teeth are so big they remind me of pieces of gum. "And I always sit next to Gina."

I shrug and then slide forward so I'm in the front row of the rug. Closer to Ms. Linhart. Lovely Ms. Linhart. She's tan with butterscotch-brown hair and tons of makeup. Also, she doesn't smile. Not *once* in the whole month since school started.

Ms. Linhart starts talking about decimals. I try to pay attention but occasionally I glance out the window. It's been raining for a week straight. Hannah says that's not typical weather for fall in Greeley. When I talked to Olivia and Lucy, they told me how they'd just spent the day on a sailboat in the bay. If I were in Captiva right now, I'd be—

"Emme," Ms. Linhart says. She flicks her long hair over her shoulder. "Where are you? Are you with us?"

I feel Gina staring hard at my back. She's the worst, but no one in my class is very nice. They either ignore me or act like I'm weird because I'm not from Greeley. No one seems to care that I have two moms. It's more like they have a problem with *me*. Like I can't seem to do anything right. Hannah is lucky she got Mr. Bryce. Whenever I walk by her classroom, everyone's laughing and chatting and listening to music.

I raise my hand.

"Yes." Ms. Linhart blinks slowly at me. "Emme?"

"Can I go to the bathroom?" I ask. I just need a minute to be alone and collect myself. Not to mention that I have to pee.

That happens when I'm nervous. I have to go every ten minutes.

"*Can* you?" Ms. Linhart asks, raising her thin eyebrows. "I certainly hope you can go to the bathroom by this point. The correct question is *may I?*"

"O.M.G." Gina says. I can hear her high-pitched giggle right behind me. Other people are laughing, too. My cheeks get warm and tears are stinging my eyes.

"Class!" Ms. Linhart says. She's frowning even *more* than usual.

"May I?" I ask quietly.

"Yes, you may." Ms. Linhart turns back to the group. "You know about adding and subtracting numbers with decimals, but what about when you multiply them?"

I push up off the rug and walk out the door. I won't cry on the way to the bathroom. I won't cry in school. I will count the seconds until lunch and recess when I see Hannah. We always eat lunch together. Sometimes a few girls from her class join us. Hands down, it's the best part of my day. Tuesdays and Thursdays are even better because those are the weekdays that we have swim team practice at the YMCA. I tried out for the Dolphins and made it. Hannah and I are both in the silver level, which is the top for our age group. On swim days, we walk home from school, have a snack, and then carpool to the Y. Today is a Tuesday, so it's Hannah's family's turn to take us.

As I'm washing my hands, I think about eating bananas with Hannah on the way to practice. Laughing in the locker room. Shrieking as we dive into the cold water. Looking at the big clock that Coach Missy props up so we can watch our times. Everything will be okay once I'm away from my class and having fun at swim practice.

When I return to the classroom, people are getting ready for gym.

"It's orienteering day so you'll be outside rain or shine," Ms. Linhart calls out. "Remember your raincoats and boots if you have them."

My teacher seems truly happy at the prospect of us orienteering (whatever that means) in a downpour. I reach into my cubby for my raincoat and slide my arms into the sleeves.

"Seriously?" Gina whispers. "A purple flowered raincoat?"

I freeze mid-zip. Is she talking to me?

"That's *so* fourth grade," Haley says.

"So not Greeley," says Alexa.

Gina, Alexa, and Haley are all wearing super-sporty black raincoats with neon-yellow stripes. I didn't get the text message that our coats need to be identical. It's not like I love my rain-coat, but who cares? It keeps me dry.

"Are you sure you're ten?" Gina asks. "You're just so . . . tiny."

I bite my lip. I can't think of a single thing to say.

"Don't get upset," Gina says. "O.M.G., we're just joking with you." Then she spins around and walks briskly into the hall.

That's it. I've had it.

As people start toward gym, I go up to Ms. Linhart. "I don't feel well. May I go to the nurse?"

Yep, *May I.*

I'm not stupid, after all.

~~~~~

"It's not a fever," Mom J says when we get home. She's obsessed with the new thermometer that she ordered. She probes it into my ear whenever I'm the least bit flushed. "And you're not queasy?"

"Not really." I set my backpack on the floor and sit on a stool in the kitchen. "I just feel . . . sick."

"Sick how?" she asks. "Does your throat hurt? I would

look down your throat but I still haven't found our flashlights. I know they're somewhere. Oh! I can use the light on my phone."

I reach down to scratch Butterball on the head.

Mom C says that if Mom J hadn't become a journalist she probably would have gone to medical school. Instead she's acting out her doctor dreams with me. I can't even tell her when I have a splinter because she'll chase me with tweezers and Neosporin.

"I'm just tired," I say, dodging her as she comes toward my throat with her phone on high beam.

I've told my moms that Ms. Linhart is strict, but that's about it. I haven't told anyone about Gina and the other girls. There's nothing anyone can do about it, and tattling on them will just make me sound like a loser. Which I'm not. Or I didn't think I was until I met Gina.

"Let's have some soup," Mom J says. "I have to finish an article after lunch and then I'm bringing ginger tea next door to Margo. You can rest in your room."

"You mean Hannah's stepmom?"

Mom J nods. "She's lovely. We have tea now and then. She works from home a few days a week."

"What do you know about Hannah's *mom*?" I ask. Hannah's never said anything about her parents getting divorced or when Margo became her stepmom.

"You mean her birth mom?" Mom J says. "Not sure."

"Yeah, that's what I meant," I say. Since I have two moms, I know all about that stuff. Mom J gave birth to me, so she's my birth mom. As soon as I was born, Mom C adopted me. I miss not having Mom C around all the time, but she loves her new job. She's a litigator. That means she's paid to argue in a courtroom. I wish I could be that brave. If I were, I'd litigate for Gina to leave me alone (and to never say "O.M.G." again).

"How is Hannah feeling about the baby?" Mom J asks as she sets a steaming bowl of chicken-noodle soup in front of me.

"What baby?" I blow on my soup. I'm feeling much better than I did an hour ago. I'm so glad I'm not at school right now.

"Margo's baby," Mom J says. "She's due in February."

I drop my spoon into my bowl. "Hannah's stepmom isn't pregnant."

"Of course she is. Haven't you noticed her belly? She's four months along."

I stare at Mom J. A few weeks ago, I asked Hannah whether she was an only child and she said yes.

"Hannah didn't tell you?"

"Nope." I slurp up some noodles. "Can I ask her about it?"

Mom J shakes salt onto cucumber spears. "Give her a chance to tell you. I bet she's still getting used to the idea."

"I guess," I say. But something about it makes me feel funny. Ever since Hannah found Butterball last month and we started hanging out, we've been telling each other *everything*.

Or so I thought.

~~~~~~

At three fifteen, the doorbell rings. I know right away it's Hannah and my heart jumps with a mix of weirdness (I'm going to give her a chance to tell me about her step-mom's pregnancy) and excitement (I have the BEST surprise for her). Hannah hasn't been to my room since the walls were painted last week.

"Emme?" Mom J calls out. "Are you awake? Hannah is coming upstairs."

"Okay," I say.

I'm sitting on my floor working on the collage that I'm doing with my cousin. After I sent my contribution of shells and shell sketches, Leesa mailed me back her addition to the tagboard. She painted a massive silvery peace symbol, which is *so* Leesa. For my turn, I'm trying to draw a picture of a baby panda. I watched a video of a panda sleeping on playground equipment at a preserve in China and it got me inspired.

"Cute panda," Hannah says, standing in my doorway. "So I didn't see you at lunch or recess or leaving school. Did you go home sick?"

"Yeah," I say, shrugging. There's no way I can tell Hannah how mean Gina and her friends are being to me. I don't want her to think she's picked the wrong person to hang out with, like I'm going to pull her down. "I didn't feel well."

"Can you still come to swim practice? We're leaving in a half hour. My dad bought some peanut butter cookies for the drive."

"Maybe," I say. "I have to ask my—"

"Hey!" Hannah says. "You painted your walls! Is it Blue Allure? It doesn't look like Sophie's room anymore, but I love it."

"Speaking of Sophie . . ." I raise my eyebrows at Hannah. *This* is the big surprise.

Hannah looks confused, so I point toward the wall by the closet, where Hannah's friend once drew a smiley face. When the painters came over, I taped around Sophie's drawing so they wouldn't paint over it. I figured it was the least I could do to thank Hannah for not being mad that I moved into Sophie's house.

"Aaaaaah!" Hannah shrieks.

"Everything okay?" Mom J calls from downstairs.

"You left Sophie's smiley face on the wall!" Hannah says.

"Everything's fine," I call down to Mom J. Then I grin at Hannah. "Do you like it? Are you surprised?"

Hannah wraps her arms around me. "Emme, I love it. It's just so *you* to do something special like that."

I smile and hug her back. After we let go, I try to figure out how to get Hannah to tell me the baby news. It's not like I can outright say, *Does anyone in your family happen to be pregnant?* Instead, as Hannah picks up the glittery wand on my desk and begins shaking it back and forth, I tip my head to one side.

"Anything new going on with you?" I ask.

Hannah twirls the wand between her fingers, the glitter and stars swirling around in the water. "Not really."

"*Nothing* at all?" I can't help feeling a little annoyed. She's got this huge thing in her life that she's not telling me. "*Everything* is the same?"

Hannah gives me a strange look and then sets the wand back on my desk. Instead of answering my question, she says, "Are you really sick? Like, do you have a cold?"

My stomach flips over when I think about what happened at school today. I guess I'm keeping something to myself, too. But it's different. A baby is good news. My teacher and the other kids in my class hating me? Not so great.

"I'm not really sick," I mutter. "I was just tired."

"Then can you come to practice? *Please?* It'll be boring without you. Pretty please with a peanut butter cup on top?"

"Let me ask my mom," I say.

I push my panda sketch aside and we both run downstairs to Mom J's office. So maybe Hannah's not ready to tell me that her stepmom is pregnant. I guess I'll have to be okay with that (for now).

"Mom J?" I clasp my hands together hopefully.

"You want to go to swim practice?" she asks, turning in her swivel chair and smiling at us. "That's the three-o'clock miracle."

"Huh?" I ask. I glance at Hannah but she just shrugs.

"That's what I call illnesses that disappear by the time school's out," Mom J says. She rolls toward me in her chair and touches my forehead. "You're still not warm. It seems like the miracle happened to you."

"I guess." I shift from one foot to the other. "So can I go?"

"Pack your wet bag," Mom J says. "Miracle child."

~~~~~

The problem is, the miracle is gone by the next morning. When I open my dresser drawers, trying to figure out what to wear to school, I feel horrible all over again. I have my regular comfy leggings and T-shirts, but what if everyone says they're *so not Greeley*? Then again, when Mom C took me back-to-school shopping, we bought sporty tees and jeans, more like what Gina and Alexa and Haley wear. But then they'll say I'm copying them.

When Mom C walks in, I'm standing in my pajamas, staring into my drawer.

"Everything okay?" she asks. "You didn't answer when I called. We're going to have breakfast before I leave for work."

"I don't feel well," I whisper, sitting on my bed.

Mom C touches the back of my neck. At least she doesn't go for the ear thermometer.

"You're not warm." Mom C sits down next to me. "Is it school? Is something happening there?"

I lean into her arm. She smells so good, like fabric softener and vanilla skin cream. I squeeze my eyes tight. And almost spill it all, about Ms. Linhart and those horrible girls. But what good would it do? Maybe three-o'clock miracles happen, but my mom can't make my entire classroom disappear.

"Do you need one more personal day?" Mom C asks.

I nod. "This'll be my last one."

"You can only read books today," Mom C says. "And not good ones. Long, boring biographies. Or write letters to Olivia and Lucy. No screen time. No panda cam. Zero fun."

She's smiling, but I know she means it. I can't keep hiding forever.

~~~~~~

Once Mom C has left for work and Mom J is in her office, I borrow Mom J's phone to call Leesa.

"Aunt Julia?" Leesa asks.

"No," I say. "It's me. Emme."

"Hey, cuz!" Leesa shouts. People are laughing in the background. I picture her on the way to breakfast at her boarding school. I try to imagine everyone wearing plaid skirts and carrying books on their hips. "What's up? Did you get the collage I sent back to you?"

"Yeah," I say, leaning back on my bed. "I love your peace symbol. Now I'm working on my part."

"Fab-amazing," Leesa says. "Rock on, crazy artist."

The thing I love about Leesa is that she's a total free spirit. She plays the ukulele and has her ears pierced seven times and she even has this strange way of talking.

"So . . . whazzup?" Leesa asks.

"I'm having a hard time at school. Don't tell my moms, okay? It's just that—"

"Other girls?" Leesa asks. "Or your teacher?"

"Both. Mostly the girls."

"Clothes? Snotty comments? Making you feel bad about yourself?"

It feels like she's reading my mind. "All of the above."

"Welcome to fifth grade. It can be a tough year. Just don't give them power. And be yourself. Keep up with the good vibes. You're my rockin' little cuz."

I pick at a scab on my knee. I don't feel very rockin'. And I have no idea what vibes have to do with any of this.

"Listen," Leesa says, "I've got to go. There's a mad dash on the French toast and I need some. Love you like crazy. Be yourself, okay? Bye!"

"I love you, too," I say, but she's already hung up.

I set down the phone and stare out the window. It's still raining out. I wonder if it's going to rain forever. I wonder if we're all going to be sucked into the gloppy mud.

Dumb mud. I smile weakly. I'll have to tell that palindrome to Hannah.

Yesterday Hannah said that leaving Sophie's smiley face on the wall was *so me*. And Leesa said to *be myself*. But here's the thing: I honestly have no idea what or who I am anymore.

five

HANNAH

W hat's *og*?" Coach Missy asks, standing above Emme and me. She's swinging a stopwatch from her wrist. She has on one blue flip-flop and one white flip-flop. That's what our coach does on meet days because those are the colors for all the teams at the YMCA, including the Dolphins.

"*Og*," I explain, "is *go* backward. So if I write *Go Emme Og*, then it's a palindrome."

Coach Missy shakes her head. "You guys are too much."

Emme and I are sitting at the edge of the pool. We've just done our freestyle and kick-swim warm-ups and now we're waiting for the meet to begin. It's the second meet of the season. Emme's swimming back and butterfly and I'm swimming two freestyles. We're also doing the medley relay together. We're wearing our crazy-tight racing suits, our team caps, and we have goggles dangling around our necks. At the moment Coach Missy finds us, we're writing on each other with black Sharpies. At swim meets everyone records event information on their arms with a marker. Lots of girls also write *Eat My Bubbles* or *Kick Kick Kick* on their shins. Emme and I decided I'd put *Go Emme Og* on my leg and she'd put *Go Hannah Og* on her leg. Lucky-charm palindromes.

"You're the Og Twins," Coach Missy says. "That's what I'm calling you from now on. I've never seen two people who are more alike. Look at your toenails!"

Emme and I tap our toes together. Once I learned that Emme always paints her toenails different colors, I started doing it, too. We currently have rainbow toes, red on the left pinkie all the way to violet on the right pinkie. We did a bunch of extra blue toenails in the middle because the rainbow only has seven colors. Maybe it seems kooky, but it makes sense to us.

"Total Og Twins," Coach Missy says, walking away.

Emme and I grin at each other. It's true that we're basically twins. We have the palindrome thing and the peanut butter thing and we live on the same street and have the same birthday and we both have sandy hair with a slight greenish hue. The only difference, really, is that I'm tall and Emme is tiny. Also, it's looking like Emme loves ice-skating, which I'm scared of. Not that I've told her that. I don't want her to think I'm a wimp.

"Are you nervous?" I ask Emme.

She shakes her head. "Not really. I just focus on one thing during the race, like kicking. What about you?"

I'm so nervous my teeth are chattering and I'm sitting on my hands to keep from chewing my nails. It doesn't help that I'm in the first heat. Also, I hate diving off the blocks. I'm always worried I'm going to fall and hit my head. I scan the bleachers. I can't see my dad and Margo. It was raining hard out, so they dropped us off at the door of the Y and circled for parking. What if they can't find parking for the whole meet and they miss all my races? I wish they'd get here already.

Emme snaps the lid onto the Sharpie. "Remember," she says, "it's just a pool loop. Get it? *Pool loop*."

"*Pool loop*," I say, nodding. "Awesome."

Coach Missy blows her whistle. "Swimmers, take your places on the blocks."

I fit my goggles in place. They're way too tight. I'm probably going to get a headache.

"Og," Emme says to me as she stands up.

"Og," I say weakly, and then walk over to lane two.

~~~~~~

The Dolphins place third in the meet, which is awesome. Even more awesome is that Emme and I both get our personal bests—Emme in the two-hundred back and me in the fifty free. Even more awesome is that our medley relay WON! We were five entire seconds ahead of the Thunderbirds.

After the meet, we all shower and change. All the girls are singing in the locker room and goofing around and celebrating our awesomeness. But then, when we come to the deck for our wrap-up meeting, we fall silent. Coach Missy is crying. She's holding her phone in one hand and dabbing her eyes with a tissue.

"I just got a text from my sister," she explains as we gather around her on the bleachers. "She lives in Deer Park. That's a few hours north, where I grew up. They've been getting even worse rain than we have this fall, and the town has flooded. They're evacuating hundreds of houses as we speak. People might lose everything."

I stare at Coach Missy. I've never seen her this upset. I have no idea what to say.

"Is there anything we can do?" Emme asks. "Like, how can we help?"

I nod along with a bunch of other girls.

Coach Missy shakes her head. "For now," she says, "just be grateful for what you have. You all did some amazing swimming today. I'm proud of all of you."

When I come down from the bleachers, my dad and Margo are waiting for me. I give them both hugs. I *am* grateful for my parents and for everything I have. Even if I do my best to ignore the fact that Margo's belly is pressing against me as she squeezes me tight.

~~~~~

On Monday, Mr. Bryce stands at the front of the rug during morning meeting. He's wearing his checkerboard tie. He's smiling and holding a big yellow envelope in each hand. They're labeled TEAM A and TEAM B. We definitely have the coolest fifth-grade teacher. Sometimes Mr. Bryce juggles balls while he's teaching. One sunny morning last week, when we *finally* got a break from the rain, he was doing read-aloud on the rug. He was reading *Holes*. He glanced toward the window and said, "Let's take this outside." He ended up reading and walking backward as we strolled from the school to

Franklin Street to Southampton Park and back again. I told Emme about it at lunch and she was so jealous. She said Ms. Linhart would never, ever do anything fun like that.

"Who's ever heard of a fund-raiser?" Mr. Bryce asks. We've finished attendance and this is the part of morning meeting where we talk about current events.

I lift my hand.

Mr. Bryce nods toward me. "Hannah?"

"It's where you raise money," I say. "Like how we have the Earth Ball and the silent auction at Greeley to raise money for the school."

"Exactly," Mr. Bryce says. "There are also fund-raisers for specific causes. Who knows some examples of causes?"

I waggle my hand again, but this time he calls on Layla. She's really nice and she's always sharing her Jelly Bellys at recess. Layla's skin is smooth and dark, and she's the tallest kid, boy or girl, in our grade. Layla and I were together in second grade, but not in third or fourth.

"A cause is something that does good things," Layla says, twisting one of her braids around her finger, "like animal rights or fighting diseases."

Mr. Bryce nods as he fires up the Smart Board. We all spring onto our knees for a closer look.

"This is Deer Park," Mr. Bryce says, scrolling past photos of submerged homes and muddy rivers gushing down streets. "It's in the Adirondacks. This past weekend, they had to evacuate over one hundred—"

"My swim coach is from there!" I blurt out. "Her sister had to evacuate on Saturday."

"Exactly, Hannah," Mr. Bryce says. "Remember to raise your hand next time."

Everyone gapes at me. It's not like I'm embarrassed that Mr. Bryce called me out. I mean, *I know someone who knows someone who lives in Deer Park*! How can I hold that in?

"People are losing everything," Mr. Bryce says. "Kids just like you suddenly don't have their clothes or beds or—"

"Or iPads," Denny blurts out.

I make a face at Denny. He has tangled rusty hair and freckles. Annoying through and through.

Marley raises her hand. "How can we help?"

Mr. Bryce grins. "Finally, what I was getting to! I called the local Red Cross. Our class is going to send money to the Deer Park families who lost their homes."

"But how will we get the money?" Layla asks.

Mr. Bryce gestures to the two envelopes in his hand. "We're going to have a fund-raiser. The class will divide into two teams. Each team will start with a ten-dollar budget. That's already in the envelope. A week from today, we'll tally our money and send it to Deer Park. We'll also have a lunch party next Friday, to celebrate."

Upon hearing that, we all cheer and stomp our feet on the rug.

Mr. Bryce grins. "Whichever team raises more money gets to pick the menu."

We cheer even louder. Denny raises his hand.

"Yes, Denny?"

"How are you going to choose teams?" Denny asks.

"Boys versus girls," Mr. Bryce says.

~~~~~~

Usually it's just Emme and me at lunch. Sometimes a few girls from my class join us. But today, all the girls in Mr. Bryce's class gather around a long table. It's me, Layla, Natalie, Marley, and a bunch of others. Emme sits next to me and unzips her lunch box. She seems quiet. I feel bad that Emme got Ms. Linhart. I know some people in that class, like Gina and Alexa, and they're really mean—the kind of girls who make you feel bad for no reason.

"Does anyone have nuts in their lunch?" Marley calls out, peering down the table at all of us.

"Are you allergic?" Emme asks.

I squeeze Emme's leg like *Don't get Marley started*, but it's too late. There's nothing Marley loves more than talking about her nut allergy.

"Anaphylactic," Marley says. "I could *literally* die if I ate a nut. It's supposed to be a nut-free cafeteria, but—"

"We know," Layla says, rolling her eyes. "No one here has nuts, right? Right. So let's talk about the fund-raiser."

Emme mouths *Sorry* to me and I shake my head like *No biggie*. I can see Emme's heat and lane times in faded Sharpie on her arm, just like mine. Also, totally by chance, we both brought leftover quesadillas for lunch. The Og Twins strike again!

Natalie dumps the contents of the yellow envelope onto the table. Sure enough, there's a ten-dollar bill. There are a few sheets of paper, including one for recording our expenses. Mr. Bryce also included an article about the Deer Park evacuations.

"We need a better name than Team A," says Layla.

"The boys are Team B?" Emme asks.

"Yeah," I say, "and we *have* to beat them. Otherwise they'll never let us forget it. I bet they'll pick pizza for the celebration lunch."

"What's wrong with pizza?" Natalie asks.

Emme and I both wrinkle our noses. It's so funny that she hates pizza as much as I do. Maybe even more. "It's so slithery," I say.

"And slimy," Emme says.

"And gross!" I conclude, laughing. Everyone is looking at us like we're crazy, but who cares? Let them eat pizza on their own time.

"So what should we do to raise money?" Natalie asks.

"We could have a lemonade stand," Marley says, "on Saturday afternoon, at Southampton Park."

"Since it's October," I say, "how about an apple-cider stand?"

"Perfect!" everyone squeals.

After some more discussion, we decide we'll use the ten dollars to buy apple cider and paper cups. It may cost more, but we all offer to contribute a little extra. We can paint a sign in the art room, and Natalie's family has a card table and a big cooler we can use.

Toward the end of lunch, I'm bouncing up and down in my chair. We're going to make so much money to send to Deer Park! I glance over at the boys. They're bashing their lunch containers together and falling out of their chairs. The yellow envelope labeled TEAM B is unopened on their table.

"How about Cider Queenz?" Emme asks. "Like, with a z at the end?"

"Love it!" Layla says, high-fiving her. "Everyone agree?"

We all nod. It's a royal name for a royally awesome team.

Emme smiles, but not her usual super-happy smile. She unscrews the cap off her apple-sauce squeeze.

"If pizza is slithery," Layla says to me, "what kind of celebration lunch are you thinking about?"

I dip my last triangle of quesadilla in the small container of salsa that I brought. "Mexican? Maybe nachos?"

We all look at Marley. Her pale face is framed by a curtain of long blond hair. "Works for me," she says, "as long as it's made in a facility without—"

"We know!" Layla says.

"Maybe you can join us for the lunch?" I ask Emme. "You can be an honorary member of the Cider Queenz."

"*If* you win." Emme zips her lunch box and sets it on her lap. Something's up. I'll have to ask her about it on the walk home from school.

"If *we* win," I say. "And we will."

~~~~~~

After school, I wait for Emme in our usual spot, but then I remember she has art club on Mondays, so I walk home by myself. Most Mondays, Uncle Peter meets me at our house because my dad and Margo work until six. But when I turn onto Centennial, I see my dad's bike in the driveway, parked right next to Margo's car.

I run across the porch and into the side door. I can't wait to tell them about the fund-raiser. I think I'll even email Coach Missy and let her know.

"Hi, Hannah," my dad says. He's at the kitchen table, sorting through mail.

Margo is leaning against the counter, drinking ginger tea. "We forgot to tell you that we'd be home early today."

I toss my backpack onto the floor. "We're going to have the coolest fund-raiser at—"

And then I see it.

It's stuck to the fridge with a magnet shaped like a green pepper. Right next to my fourth-grade school picture, there's a small, grainy, black-and-white image of a baby kicking his feet straight up in the air. No, not a baby. An alien with a giant head and spindly legs.

"That's him," Margo says. "We just got back from the ultrasound."

"Him?" I ask. I'm having one of those moments where my legs are weak and I can barely hear my own voice.

"It's a boy," my dad says, pointing to the fridge. "That's your baby brother."

I run up to my room and slam the door.

~~~~~

Hours later, after I've sulked through dinner and slacked through homework and rushed through a two-second shower, I go to bed. But I can't fall asleep. I try to think about the kids who lost their homes in Deer Park and how lucky I am to be in my own bed. But instead I keep thinking about the big-headed alien baby on our fridge.

I crawl out of bed, slip down to the kitchen, snatch up the

picture, and carry it to my room. I slide it into the drawer of my bedside table, far out of sight.

~~~~~

In the morning, Margo and my dad look at me a little funny, but neither of them say a word about the missing picture of the alien baby.

"Did you realize we were supposed to go to a tropical island this February?" I ask as I'm shaking cereal into my bowl. "Remember the Bahamas?"

My dad glances at Margo. She was spooning yogurt into a bowl but she pauses in midair.

"Since we're not doing that, I've been thinking about New York City," I say. "Wouldn't it be cool to visit? Like at Christmas?"

I know I'm being bratty, but I wasn't the one who decided to stick an ultrasound picture to the fridge.

"Plans change," my dad says, sighing.

~~~~~

The next day, during art class, we get permission to paint the sign. The Cider Queenz crowd around a big table, paint-brushes in hand. We write:

The Cider Queenz of Mr. Bryce's class present:
Cold Apple Cider*
One Dollar
All proceeds benefit the victims of the flood
in Deer Park, NY
*Made in a facility without nuts

We're painting rainbow-colored cups at the bottom of the paper when a few boys saunter by.

"An apple-cider stand?" Max asks. He's Denny's best buddy. *Ick* by association.

"Yeah," says Layla. "At Southampton Park on Saturday afternoon."

"Yeah, right, you're *queens*. Just like I'm a duke." Denny smirks at our sign. "Isn't a dollar a little expensive?"

"And what's up with the nut thing?" Max asks. "Who makes apple cider with nuts?"

"You never know," Marley says, pulling her long blond hair into a ponytail. "Besides, do you guys have any clue what you're doing for the fund-raiser?"

Max and Denny snort. As they're walking away, Denny turns and says, "That's for us to know and you to find out."

"Oh, *yeah*," Max says.

"More like for YOU to find out!" Layla calls back to them.

The Cider Queenz crack up. And then, before I can stop myself, I shout, "Bow to the queens because it looks like we're having Mexican food for that party! *Mmmmm.* I can already taste the guacamole."

~~~~~

After breakfast on Saturday morning my dad tells me that we're riding our bikes to swim practice. It's sunny out and sixty, with a wisp of burning leaves in the air. A perfect day for an apple-cider stand. The Cider Queenz are meeting at Southampton Park at two. Mr. Bryce even said he'd try to come by.

"What about Emme?" I ask as my dad pulls on his stretchy bike shirt. "Aren't we carpooling to practice?"

"I already talked to her moms and they're taking her today," my dad says. "I'd like to get some time with you. Grab your helmet."

There are paved bike paths that run all the way through Greeley. They're like little versions of roads with mini traffic signs and stoplights and yellow lines. It's two miles to the Y. As I'm cycling, I think about how biking is like swimming, the way you get into your own quiet groove. Then again, sometimes I wonder if I'm actually a team-sport person, like how I love volleyball in gym. Layla and Marley have invited me to play volleyball at the Y with them, but I'm always at swim practice so I can never do it.

"Hannah?" my dad says, pulling up next to me.

I ease my bike closer to the curb so there's room for both of us.

"I thought this might be a good time to talk," my dad says. "About the baby. About the other day."

I don't say a word as I focus on the road. There's a YIELD sign up ahead.

My dad clears his throat. "If you don't want the ultrasound picture on the fridge, we understand. We understand this is hard for you and sometimes you don't have words for the emotions you're feeling. We also understand that there's a lot going on, with Sophie moving and the adoption and a new sibling at the same time."

I start pedaling harder. I know my dad is saying important stuff. But when I try to make sense of it, it sounds like *wah wah waaaaaah*. Also, it's not like I agreed to a deep, meaningful conversation right now.

"No matter what happens," my dad says, "even when this little boy is born, you will always be our wonderful child, too. We will never forget that."

I pedal even faster. My heart is pounding and my legs are burning. My dad gets the hint and falls back behind me.

~~~~~

A little before two, Margo drives Emme and me to Southampton Park with our jugs of apple cider. She drops us off at the curb and we make a plan for her to pick us up when the stand is over.

"Are you sure it's okay I'm coming?" Emme asks as we're walking up the hill to meet the other Cider Queenz. "It's not like I'm in Mr. Bryce's class."

"Of course it's okay!" I pause to shift the jugs in my arms.

"But what if people ask why I'm here?" Emme asks. "Won't it seem weird?"

"Who would even ask that?"

Emme stares down at the ground. "I don't know," she mumbles. "Gina or Alexa."

I make a face. "Who cares about Gina and Alexa? They're annoying. They're probably at home annoying someone else. Besides, *you* thought of our team name. You have to come."

"I have to pee," Emme says quietly. "I'll meet you at the top of the hill."

When I get to the grassy clearing, Natalie and her dad are setting up the card table, and this other girl, Brianna, is taping on our sign. I put my cider into the cooler next to the jugs that are already in there. Emme shows up a minute later and we help lay out cups and copies of the article about Deer Park. By two on the dot, we are open for business.

"We look awesome," Layla declares, offering Emme and me pieces of gum.

I unwrap the gum and pop it in my mouth. "We *are* awesome."

Before long, people start buying cider. When a man walking his dog sees the article about the evacuations, he tucks a five-dollar bill into our jar.

"Take *that*, Team B," Marley says, giggling.

We sell twenty cups of cider in thirty minutes. We've already paid back the ten dollars from our budget and made fifteen dollars more. If we're here for a few hours, we're going to make so much money to send to Deer Park!

But then something strange happens. People stop coming to our stand. We wait. We restack the cups. Finally, Layla and I decide to tour Southampton Park to see what's up. We go down the hill, past the basketball courts, and over toward the playground. And then we see it.

"Oh my . . ." Layla says.

My mouth drops open. "No. Way."

There, right at the entrance to the playground, are the boys from Mr. Bryce's class. They're gathered around a table with a messy sign taped to the front. On the sign, they've scribbled:

The CIDER DUX best APPLE CIDER!
CHEAP! NO NUTS!!!!

No pictures or anything. Even so, their stand is buzzing with customers. The boys are hustling around, handing out cups of cider, acting like it's the most original idea in the world.

"Cider *Dux?*" I say to Layla. I can feel my hands curling into fists. "Like *ducks?*"

"I think they meant *dukes* except they got it wrong," Layla says. "They were trying to be cool, like us, the way we have a *z* at the end. But they should have spelled it *D-O-O-X.*"

"Dukes, ducks," I say, shaking my head. "I can't believe

they're selling apple cider, too! They can't do that!" I spit my gum into a trash can. "Besides, why do they have so many customers? They're selling way more than us."

Before Layla can answer, Denny lifts a megaphone to his mouth. "Cold cider! Only fifty cents! The best deal in Southampton Park! Made without nuts!"

Layla and I push through the crowd until we're face-to-face with Denny, who is wearing a plastic gold crown.

"Looks like you came up with an original idea," I snarl.

Layla smacks her hands on her hips. "What exactly is going on here?"

"Yeah, *ducks*," I say. "What's going on?"

"*Dukes*, if you please." Denny takes off his crown and bows his head. "We're raking it in."

"Oh, *yeah*," Max says, shaking the glass jar of money. "Big-time bucks."

A bunch of the guys laugh and nod along with him. This one kid, Micah, flashes us the peace sign.

"But you can't do this," I say. I glance at their card table. They've pre-poured their apple cider into paper cups, rows and rows of cups filled with cider, just waiting to be sold to *our customers*! "You stole our idea and you're charging less."

A woman with three runny-nosed boys hands Denny a dollar fifty. Denny thanks her and then instructs Max to give her three cups.

"All's fair in fund-raising," Denny says. Then he plucks a cup of cider off the table, guzzles it in one sip, and wipes his upper lip. "Looks like the Dukes are picking pizza for the victory lunch. Pizza to eat, pizza to drink, and pizza for dessert. Hail to the Cider Dukes."

I've had it. I'm so angry at Denny, at the Cider *Ducks*, at boys in general. Even my dad, for trying to have a deep, meaningful conversation on the bike ride this morning. And, of course, I'm mad at the little alien boy for just *being*.

I reach behind Denny, grab a cup of apple cider, and splash it at his shirt. Brown liquid spreads out across his chest. As Denny stands there, shocked, Layla lets out a huge squeal.

"The Cider Queenz rule!" she says. Then she picks up another cup of cider and chucks it at Denny. This time it hits the front of his shorts.

Max and the other guys look at Denny, wet with cider, and start laughing like crazy.

"Looks like someone's had an accident," Micah snorts, pointing to Denny's soaked shorts.

"Way to back me up," Denny snaps. He reaches over and dumps a cup of cider right on top of Micah's head.

"What the—" Micah blinks as he pushes his damp hair out of his face.

The people who'd been waiting in line for cider quickly grab their bags and scooters and hurry away. I hear someone say they're going to go find the adults in charge. A man wearing a backward baseball cap says, "You all should be ashamed of yourselves."

Micah reaches for a cup of cider and throws it at Denny, and with that it's an all-out cider war. It's not even girls versus boys. I'm throwing cider at Denny and Denny is throwing cider at Layla and me, and Max and Micah pour cider on another boy's head. But then Layla aims for Max and by mistake sprays cider all over my arm.

"I'm so sorry!" she shrieks.

But I barely hear her. Because I can see Denny gathering several cups together on the table.

"No way," I hiss to him.

Some parents are hurrying over. I have to act fast if I want to clear the entire table. I mean, really finish this thing. I reach out my arm—but when Denny sees what I'm about to do, he grabs my wrist.

"Hey!" he says. "You can't do that! This is all the cider we've got!"

His hands are so wet that I easily wriggle out of his grasp. "All's fair in fund-raising!" I say, tipping the paper cups like dominos. By this point, empty cups are scattered everywhere and cider is dripping all over the pavement.

But then everyone gets quiet. Mr. Bryce is walking toward us, frowning. My knees go weak. I pull back my arms, but I mistakenly knock over two more cups. One splashes my leg and the other falls on Denny's sneakers.

"The fund-raiser is canceled," Mr. Bryce says sternly. "Clean up immediately."

At the exact same time, Denny and I say, "But—"

"We'll discuss it on Monday," Mr. Bryce says. Then he shakes his head, turns around, and gets into a huddle with several of the parents.

I kick at a cup under my foot. I am soaked with cider. I reek of cider. I am never drinking cider again for the rest of my life. And it's all the boys' fault.

six

EMME

I didn't think Hannah would want to come to Landon's Organic Apple Orchard with us on the first Thursday in November. Swim practice is canceled today but Hannah and apples aren't the best of friends. It's been two weeks since the Queenz-versus-Dux fight and she still won't drink cider. I don't blame her. When she and Layla came back up the hill, dripping with cider, and told us what had happened, we were stunned. We hovered around, hugging Hannah and Layla, wiping them off with paper towels and trying to get them to stop crying. Marley kept saying how shocked she was, like what if someone in the crowd had been allergic to cider and then got doused with it? I felt so bad for Hannah, but in a way it was nice to be part of a class where the girls get along and stick up for each other. Which is basically the opposite of my class.

This afternoon Landon's is having an apple festival. They're giving away free cider and donuts, and Mom J and I are planning to pick a ton of apples. When we first moved up here I rolled my eyes at Mom J's apple-picking passion, but I've found that it's fun to climb ladders and pull apples from stems and make pies and stew applesauce. I love the way the house smells like cinnamon even the next day.

Mom J invited Hannah and Margo to join us. They were excited about it even though Hannah made sure to say that she'd *for sure* skip the cider. Margo told Mom J that they hadn't been apple-picking this entire year, which is funny because we're so dorky about our first fall in the Northeast that we've gone picking five times. I guess it's the same as how we lived in Florida my whole life and never went to Disney World (for real!).

As Mom J is driving down Centennial, she glances into the backseat at Hannah. "Speaking of apples, I heard you had some drama with cider at that fund-raiser," she says with a smile.

"Mom!" I hiss. She can be so embarrassing. The other day she tried to kiss me when she dropped me off at school. Of

course Alexa and Haley were walking in the front door *that very second* so I nudged her away. Even so, I could see them elbowing each other and cracking up.

"Let's just say that Hannah soaked the competition," Margo says, laughing.

Hannah grins and flashes me a thumbs-up. "Cider bath."

I smile back at her. It's good to see she can laugh about it now.

"What did your teacher do?" Mom J asks. "Mr. Bryce, right?"

"Be careful or she'll write an article about you," I whisper to Hannah.

"Off the record," Mom J says, flicking her blinker.

Hannah shrugs. "We all got a lecture and had to apologize to each other. Then Mr. Bryce made us think of a way to work together to raise more money. It was actually fun."

"I wish I had Mr. Bryce," I say, sighing. When Hannah's class had a bake sale the following week, I bought the yummiest Rice Krispies Treat. I even ordered it from Denny, who let me look them over and pick the biggest one. "I can't stand Ms. Linhart."

"Really?" Margo asks.

Hannah's stepmom is wearing a loose sweatshirt and

rubbing her palm around on her belly. It's so obvious she's pregnant and yet Hannah still hasn't said anything about it.

"She's really strict," I explain. "She made us miss recess last week. And that was just because we didn't finish our writing fast enough. She said we were all talking, except it was only two people. I think she's Ms. *Cold*hart."

Mom J glances into the rearview mirror at me. I haven't come home sick anymore, but I'm not skipping happily to school every morning, either. Sometimes when I can't stand being in class I tell Ms. Linhart I have a stomachache and then I go to the nurse. But most days I just have to deal.

"Ms. *No*hart," Hannah offers.

"Exactly," I say.

And don't even get me started on those girls in my class. They make Ms. Linhart look as sweet as hot apple pie.

~~~~

When we get home, Mom J and I haul our bags of apples into the kitchen. As Butterball sniffs the apples, Mom J takes a picture and texts it to Mom C. We must have picked fifteen pounds!

"Do you want to talk about Ms. Linhart?" Mom J asks. "It sounds like things aren't going so well at—"

"What's that?" I say, pointing to a padded envelope on the counter.

Changing the subject. Number *two* way of diverting Mom J from a cross-examination (number one is to say I feel feverish). The last thing I want to do is talk about school and how no one in my class likes me. I live it all day. No need to relive the misery at night.

"It's from Leesa," Mom J says. "It arrived this morning."

I grab the envelope and tear it open. My cousin finally mailed me our ongoing collage. It took her *forever!* Back in October, I couldn't get my panda drawing just right. Instead, I ironed a fall leaf inside wax paper, glued it onto the tagboard, and sent the collage to her dorm at boarding school. (Yep, the rusty orange leaf is me being a geek about my first fall in the Northeast.)

As soon as I see what Leesa added to the collage, I can't stop laughing. It was totally worth the wait.

~~~~~

The next day, my class is pin-drop quiet during math and we all show our work and we even finish our questions early. Ms. Linhart decides to be human and grace us with ten minutes of choice time before gym. Most people grab books or gather together at tables, talking and laughing. I go to my cubby and pull out the collage from Leesa. I've already decided I'm going to draw bubble letters saying *The Good Vibes Cousins*, slather it in glitter, and mail it back to her. If I can get the letters sketched out now, I'll swing by the art room after school and use their assortment of glitter glue.

I pull the collage out of the envelope and start laughing all over again. I don't know where Leesa found this, but she's stuck on a photograph of a highway restaurant with a sign out front that says CHILDREN WITH GAS EAT FREE. Obviously it's supposed to mean that if you fill your tank, your kids get a meal. But it sounds like farting children eat for free.

"Emme?" Gina asks.

I whip my head around. Gina is peering at me. Her eyes are so pale they look like they've been left to dry in the sun.

"What?" I ask hoarsely. My heart starts pounding in my chest.

Gina tips her head to one side. "Were you just, like, talking to yourself?"

"I was . . ." I quickly slide the collage back into the envelope. The last thing I want is for Gina to see my project with my cousin or to know anything about me. "I was laughing."

"O.M.G., she *was* talking to herself," Gina announces to Alexa and Haley, who rush over as soon as they see Gina with me.

Alexa flashes her tremendous teeth. "You're kind of weird?"

I'm not sure if she's asking a question or stating a fact. Either way, it's not a compliment. My face flushes and I stare down at the floor.

"We're just joking," Gina says, touching my arm.

"O.M.G.," Alexa says.

I want to pull away from Gina, but I'm stuck. Completely stuck.

"What's in there anyway?" Gina asks. She lets go of me and snatches my padded envelope up off the table.

"*No,*" I plead. My throat is so tight it comes out like a whisper.

As Gina sticks her hand into the envelope, I reach out to grab it back from her, but it's no use. She's already yanked out the collage and she's turning away from me, holding it out for Haley and Alexa to see.

"Oh my god!" Gina says to them. "A leaf in wax paper? Didn't we do that in kindergarten? A peace sign? Drawings of shells?" Gina shoves the tagboard into Haley's hands, like it's so far beneath her she doesn't even want to touch it. "Is this, like, a joke?"

"It's just something . . . my cousin . . ." I pause. My cheeks are burning hot and tears are stinging my eyes. Why am I even trying to explain myself to Gina? "It's nothing," I finally say.

Haley pokes Gina's arm. "Look at this about children with gas."

"Gross!" Alexa squeals.

"Here's a helpful hint," Gina says, leaning down so her face is really close to mine. Her breath smells like warm Doritos. "Grow up."

As Gina pulls back from me, I'm literally in shock. I can't believe this is happening.

"We're not getting to you, are we?" Haley asks. She glances at Ms. Linhart's desk and smiles sweetly. Ms. Linhart nods back at her like nothing is going on. "You don't mind, right?"

"Right?" Gina asks. She brushes her fingers over my shoulder. "I mean, we're just trying to be helpful."

I nod slowly. It's all I can do not to cry.

As soon as they walk away, I go over to the water shelf, where we keep our bottles. I face the wall and take a few deep breaths as I sip my water. Part of me doesn't want to let them win. I might even go back to my table and get the collage out and write *The Good Vibes Cousins* just like I planned to do before they made fun of it. I bet that's what Leesa would do— be strong and be herself no matter what.

I return to my table. I won't even let myself look at Gina or the other girls as I take the collage out of the envelope.

But then I see it.

Someone has written *LOSER* in bold black letters across the top of the collage.

LOSER.

I look across the classroom. A bunch of kids are huddled around Gina, Alexa, and Haley. They're all whispering and giggling and covering their mouths with their hands.

I crumple the collage into the envelope and head up to Ms. Linhart's desk. She's marking up our math work with a red pen.

"I need to go to the nurse," I say.

"Again?" she asks, pressing her lipsticked lips together. "You seem to be very fond of the nurse."

I don't even answer. I just walk out.

On the way down the hall, I toss the envelope and the collage into a trash bin.

"Emme, are you okay?" Hannah asks as she parts the pea-green curtain around the cot in the back of the nurse's office.

I'm sitting cross-legged on the cot, tears trickling down my face, a tissue scrunched in my fist, unsure how I'll ever walk back into Ms. Linhart's class. Everyone in there thinks I'm a LOSER. The nurse offered to call my moms, but I knew that would start a cross-examination, so I just said I had a headache and needed to rest.

"How did you know I was here?" I ask.

"Marley told me," Hannah says, sitting next to me. "She was delivering a new EpiPen to the nurse and saw you coming in and said you looked upset. Are you okay?"

I consider telling Hannah that I have a headache (not true) or that I hate Ms. Linhart (true). Instead I bite my bottom lip and then say, "Can I tell you the real truth?"

"For the Og Twins?" Hannah says, squeezing my hand. "Always."

My hands are sweaty, but Hannah never lets go as I tell her about Gina and Alexa and Haley and how they're so mean to me and how the rest of the kids ignore me and how Ms. Linhart makes it even worse. I even tell Hannah what someone (I'm guessing Gina) wrote on the collage and how I threw it away.

When I'm done talking, my face is wet and my nose is running, but I feel a little better. I had no idea I was holding so much inside.

"Oh, Emme," Hannah says, hugging me. "What are we going to do? We need to tell your moms."

"I've thought about that and there's nothing anyone can do."

"How do you know?"

"It'll just make things worse. It's not like I want Ms. Linhart going around the classroom trying to get someone to confess that they wrote *LOSER* about me. Everyone will deny it and I'll look even more like a loser."

"But what if it's not just about the collage?" Hannah asks. "What if you say that people have been mean to you for months?"

I shake my head. "Then Ms. Linhart will hate me even more, like I'm accusing her of letting this go on. Gina and the rest of them will make fun of me for telling."

"I see what you mean," Hannah says. "But it's just so . . ."

"Awful," I say, blowing my nose.

I glance around the little room with only a cot, a box of tissues, and a barf basin on the floor. They had the same barf basin at the nurse's office on Captiva Island. But back in Captiva, I was actually sick when I went to the nurse. I wasn't hiding out.

"Can I tell *you* the real truth about something?" Hannah says, chewing at her thumbnail.

"For the Og Twins?" I blot my eyes. "Of course."

Hannah leans in close to me and whispers, "Margo's pregnant. My dad and Margo are having a baby."

I'm so relieved she finally told me that I smile.

"What's so funny?" Hannah asks.

"It's just . . ." I pause. I'm not sure how to tell her this.

"Kind of obvious?"

"Yeah," I say, exhaling. "She's huge. She looks like she's going to have the baby any day now."

"Not until February," Hannah says quickly. "*Late* February."

I can tell she looks upset so I squeeze her hand back.

"I'm sorry I didn't tell you before," Hannah says. "Plus, there's this other thing going on."

As Hannah pauses, I think about how we're in the nurse's office and the phone keeps ringing and there's a barf bucket (with a weird brownish stain in it) on the floor and yet it actually feels cozy and safe in here. I had good friends in Captiva, Olivia and Lucy, but we've been talking less and less since I moved. And really, I feel closer to Hannah than I ever was to them.

"The thing is," Hannah says, "Margo is adopting me."

I totally didn't see that coming. "She's *adopting* you? But what about your—"

"Real mom?"

"Birth mom," I say. "Margo is your real mom."

Hannah nods like she hadn't thought about that before. "My, uh, birth mom never wanted kids," she says quietly. "She gave me up to my dad when I was born. I've never talked about that to anyone before. Not even Sophie."

Mom C says I always have a comment or question about everything. But at this moment, I can't think of a single thing to say.

"They've been working on the adoption for a while," Hannah says. "It's going to be finalized soon. We're waiting for a court date any day now."

"Wow," I say. "Congratulations."

"I guess." Hannah sits on her hands and rocks side to side. "I'm scared, though."

"Me too," I say.

"I'm glad we're Og Twins," Hannah says. "I feel like this is what it means to be best friends. To tell each other things we wouldn't tell anyone else."

Best friends. I've been thinking it. She said it. *Best friends.*

"Me too," I say.

Hannah stretches out her foot and kicks the barf basin under the cot.

"I couldn't look at that for one more second," she says, laughing.

~~~~~

The next day is Saturday and we practice hard. Coach Missy has us do the usual warm-ups of freestyle, backstroke, and freestyle again. Then we get into kicking with the board while she's timing us, which is brutal for me because my legs are short (I'm much better when it's all about the arms). Then Coach Missy has us do breast and free sprints with descends, which means our times have to be faster with each lap.

By the end of practice, my upper arms are sore and my neck is stiff. I stand under the shower for several minutes, trying to decide what I want to do when I get home. Eat (I'm so hungry) or sleep (I'm so tired). Or can I eat and sleep at the same time?

"Too hot to hoot!" Hannah sings when I finally wrap myself in a towel and meet her at the lockers. She's dressed and packing her wet bag.

"Huh?" I ask.

Hannah snaps her goggles at me, but they hit a locker instead. "You're *too hot to hoot*. A palindrome."

"Ah." I grab my heap of clothes, sit on a bench, and start getting dressed. It's not easy to tug on clothes under a towel but that's how we do it. "I'm just glad I got through those sprints."

"And I'm glad practice is over," Hannah says. She looks in the mirror and attempts to gather her hair into a ponytail. I've noticed that it's started to get longer. "I didn't want to come today."

"Why not?" I ask. As much as it can be exhausting, I still love swim practice.

"Volleyball is so much more fun," Hannah says. She shakes her hair around her shoulders again. "So is basketball. So is eating. Did I tell you I heard about a restaurant in New York City that specializes in peanut butter? Cinnamon peanut butter . . . maple peanut butter . . . spicy peanut—"

"I'm so hungry!" I say. "Don't talk about peanut butter right now."

We both laugh and then hurry into the lobby of the YMCA to meet her dad.

After lunch, I'm in my room when Hannah knocks on the door and then walks right in. That's typical for us these days. We're always running back and forth between each other's houses.

"What's up?" I say. I finally unpacked my ribbons from my swim meets in Captiva and I'm hanging them above my bed. I was going to use nails, but Mom C suggested thumbtacks instead.

"Cool ribbons," Hannah says. "That's a lot of firsts."

"Mostly breaststroke. Some medleys, too." It's true that I've placed first a lot. People say that if you want to be a serious swimmer you have to be tall with long arms and legs, but being short hasn't hurt me so far.

"So," Hannah says, handing me a thumbtack. "I've been thinking about it and we have to tell your moms."

I turn to her. Is she saying what I think she's saying? "Tell them what?"

"About what's going on at school." Hannah gestures toward the door. "Like . . . now."

I shake my head quickly. I seriously don't want to do this.

"You can do it, Emme." She points to my neat row of ribbons. "You're a winner."

I feel like the opposite of a winner. But I also get what Hannah is saying and so I set a second-place ribbon (breaststroke, twenty-five meters) back in the shoe box, run into the bathroom to pee, and then follow her downstairs.

Mom J and Mom C are in the backyard, digging holes to plant bulbs. They've become obsessed with daffodil bulbs and tulip bulbs and how you have to plant them in the ideal location on the ideal day in the fall with the ideal low-nitrogen fertilizer.

As Hannah pushes open the back door, I drag slowly behind her. I think I have to pee again.

"Claire? Julia?" Hannah says.

Mom J wipes her hands on her jeans and looks over at Mom C, who leans her shovel against the tree. "What's up?"

"Maybe we can all sit down," Hannah says, steering me toward the picnic table. "Something's going on at school. With Emme."

As we slide into the table, I keep telling myself *you're a winner, you're a winner.* But I'm definitely feeling more like a loser, just like they wrote on the collage.

"The thing is," Hannah says, "Ms. Linhart is terrible. And some girls in Emme's class are being awful to her. Gina and Alexa and Haley. I know them and they're all really mean. They're making fun of Emme. They even ruined her collage. They wrote something bad on it."

"Oh, Emme," Mom J says. "Have you told anyone? Why didn't you tell us?"

I glance at Hannah and she nods encouragingly. "There's nothing you can do about it," I say quietly. "I told Hannah. And I told Leesa a little."

"What did Leesa say?" Mom J asks.

"To be true to myself," I say. "And to keep up the good vibes."

This time Mom C gives Mom J a look. Leesa is Mom C's older sister's daughter. I think she drives both my moms a little crazy.

"Does Ms. Linhart know?" Mom C asks. "Have you talked about it with her?"

"No," I say. "But she has to see it."

"What did they do to the collage?" Mom C asks.

I shake my head. I don't want to say it out loud. "It's over. I already threw it away."

Mom J clears her throat and then sits up straight. "First of all," she says in her no-nonsense lawyer voice, "thank you,

Hannah, for looping us in. There's a lot we can do. You're talking to a journalist and a litigator, as well as two moms who would do anything to fight for their kid."

I bite the insides of my cheeks. "But I don't want to fight," I say. "It'll just make it worse."

"When Mom C says *fight*," Mom J explains, "she doesn't mean we're going to actually *fight*. She means we'll stand up for you. It can be a quiet kind of fighting. There's more than one way to skin a cat."

We all look over at Butterball, scratching his claws against a wooden fence at the edge of the yard.

"Don't say that!" Hannah shouts. "What if Butterball understands people language?"

"He'll be traumatized for life," I say, attempting to smile.

~~~

By Sunday night, everything is different.

I can't believe it. I really can't.

After dinner, Mom J and Mom C invite Hannah over for homemade crumble-top apple pie. As Mom J passes out forks and Mom C scoops vanilla ice cream onto our plates, Hannah hands me a blue ribbon that she's made from construction paper. It says *First Place* in silver marker.

"For your wall," Hannah says. "It's the most artistic thing I've done all year."

"First-place *what*?" I ask.

Hannah tugs her hair into a ponytail. This time she gets most of it into the rubber band. "Whatever kind of winner you want," she says.

I grin at Hannah. Because right now I *do* feel like a winner.

After our talk yesterday, Mom C emailed the principal and the guidance counselor at Greeley Elementary and arranged an emergency phone meeting. They even had Ms. Linhart on the call at some point. When I heard that, it made me so nervous my hands were shaking. At first, the guidance counselor said she could have a talk with Gina and the others on Monday, which my moms said definitely needed to happen. Even so, my moms didn't want me in a classroom with them anymore.

This morning, the principal called to say I'm being switched to Ms. Chung's fifth-grade class. Effective *tomorrow*! Mr. Bryce's class doesn't have room but there's a girl from swim team, Jillian, who has Ms. Chung and says she's really nice.

"This pie is so good," Hannah says, balancing an enormous

bite on her fork. "I can't believe we picked these apples ourselves."

Mom J smiles at Hannah. "Thank you again for watching out for Emme. I'm so glad you both came to us."

"Of course," Hannah says, her mouth full of pie. "The thing is, Emme is . . ."

As Hannah chews and swallows, I know she's going to say it.

"'Too hot to hoot?" I ask, grinning.

Hannah laughs so hard she starts coughing and has to chug her entire glass of milk. "That's exactly what I was going to say!"

Mom C shakes her head. "Sometimes I feel like you girls speak your own language."

Hannah and I look at each other and shrug. I guess we sort of do.

Later, as I'm walking Hannah across the yard, we make a plan for tomorrow morning. Mom J is coming along to meet with the principal, and Hannah says she'll go into Ms. Chung's class with me. I'm nervous about starting in a new class in November, but anything is better than facing Ms. Linhart's room again.

We reach Hannah's side porch. "Remember what you told me?" I ask, hugging my arms around my chest. It's getting wintery cold out, and I'm just wearing a sweatshirt and jeans. "About how Margo is adopting you?

Hannah nods. She's got a jacket on, but she squeezes her arms around her chest, too.

"I realized something," I say. "We're both going to have one birth parent and one adoptive parent."

It's dark out, but I can see by the porch light that Hannah is staring at me.

"My mom Julia had me and my mom Claire adopted me," I explain.

When Hannah breathes, a puff of cold air comes out of her mouth. "Og Twins," she says quietly.

"Forever," I say.

Then we both dash into our houses.

seven

HANNAH

I aim, leap, and shoot the basketball from the end of the driveway. Of course I miss.

"R!" Uncle Peter shouts, scooping up the ball and dribbling it around in triumphant circles.

"No fair!" I shriek, but I'm totally smiling.

It's Thursday after school and Uncle Peter and I are playing H-O-R-S-E in the driveway. It's not that cold for early December, maybe high forties, and we're running around so much that I'm getting warm in my hoodie.

Uncle Peter shoots again, but he misses.

"Your turn, Hannah Banana," he says, grinning as he passes the ball to me. I love spending time with my uncle. He's my dad's younger brother. He's a blonder, goofier version of my dad. He doesn't have kids of his own, so I'm the closest he's got. Usually he watches me on Mondays, but Margo has an appointment with her obstetrician, which is a doctor that takes care of pregnant women, so she switched him to Thursday.

I dribble the ball over to my sweet spot. It's right under the hoop, a little to the left. When I shoot from here I get a basket almost every time. Because of this, my uncle already has an *H*. The way H-O-R-S-E works is that you shoot from a certain location. If you get a basket, your opponent has to shoot and make it from that exact same spot. If they don't make it, they get a letter from the word *horse*. Whoever gets *H-O-R-S-E* first loses. The problem is, Uncle Peter is over six feet tall and he shows no mercy. Whenever it's his turn, he'll shoot from way far away. That's how I have my *H* and *O* and now this latest *R*. This time, though, I'm determined to beat him.

I aim, shoot, and . . . sink it right through the hoop.

"Score!" I shout, tossing the ball to my uncle. "Bet you can't do *that*!"

"Hannah?" Emme calls from her driveway. "Ready for swim practice?"

"Hey, Emme!" Uncle Peter says as he dribbles the ball back and forth under his knees. Show-off.

Emme waves at Uncle Peter. She's wearing her brand-new puffy blue parka and blue hat and blue gloves. Emme and her moms are so excited about their first winter in Greeley that they all bought new coats and they hung stockings from their mantel even before Thanksgiving. I was teasing Emme about it until she pointed out that I've been talking nonstop about how I want to go to New York City at Christmas and see the tree at Rockefeller Center. Oh, and maybe stop by that peanut-butter restaurant.

"You should probably get your swim stuff," Emme says. "My mom is coming out to the car in a second."

"I . . . uhhh." I fiddle with the zipper on my sweatshirt. "I don't think I'm going to practice today."

I glance at Uncle Peter, but he just shrugs. "Your decision. Or do you want me to text your parents and ask?"

I quickly shake my head. We shouldn't bother them when they're at the obstetrician. *Ugh.* They're talking about the baby more and more now, and they've started making lists of names. They told me I can pick his middle name, but I'm not sure I want to. It's not that I have anything against babies. I like them as much as the next person. But they scream and puke and poop and then their parents whisk them away from you and *take them home*. They don't live in *your house*, where you've been an only child for almost eleven years.

"You're not coming?" Emme asks. She pulls off a glove, tears open the wrapper of a cereal bar, and takes a bite.

I pinch a rubber band out of my jeans pocket and twist my hair into a ponytail. I've decided I'm going to grow my hair out this year. I've always kept it short because of swimming, so it'll dry quickly and won't be bulky under my cap. But I'm sick of it. I want to have long hair for once in my life.

"I'm going to skip practice," I say.

"Won't Coach Missy be upset?" Emme asks.

"It's one day," I say. "She won't even notice."

"Okay." Emme shifts her weight from one foot to the other. "Well . . . see you later."

As soon as she's gone, Uncle Peter tries to get a basket from my sweet spot. Not even close.

"*Oh!*" I shout to him. "I got you so bad!"

He tries another shot from the end of the driveway. This time he misses.

"Yes!" I shriek, diving for the ball. "Yesssss!"

~~~

When my parents pull into the driveway a half hour later, we're still playing basketball.

"What happened to swim practice?" Margo asks me.

"I wasn't in the mood," I say.

Uncle Peter flashes a lopsided grin. "How can I say no to my niece?"

"How's the alien baby?" I ask them both. That'll change the subject.

My dad smiles. "He's still orbiting."

I guess it's a slight improvement that we can joke about the baby now. Sometimes, when I'm alone, I take the ultrasound picture out of my drawer and wonder what he will actually look like. Maybe his middle name can be Alien.

Later that afternoon, once Uncle Peter has left, we're all in the kitchen. I'm multiplying fractions at the table. Margo and my dad are making burgers. Other than avoiding onions, Margo's all-day sickness seems to be better. At least peanut butter is allowed in the house again.

Margo sets some carrot sticks on the table next to me. "Honey," she says, pouring a puddle of ranch dressing on my plate to use as dip, "we heard from the lawyer today. Remember Ryan? We got the court date."

I was just transporting a carrot stick from the plate into my mouth. I drop it onto my homework page and stare up at them.

My dad nods and says, "It's going to be two weeks from yesterday. We'll take you out of school for the day."

Two weeks from yesterday, I will be in a courtroom with a judge and a lawyer and who knows how many other people. Two weeks from yesterday, Margo will be adopting me.

I reach over to pick up my carrot stick but accidentally grab my pencil and swipe the eraser through the ranch dressing. At least I caught myself before taking a bite.

~~~~~~

On Saturday morning, I try to get out of swim practice again. I just don't feel like going back and forth in the pool fifty thousand times. But despite my protests, Margo is firm.

"You missed on Thursday," she says as she hands me my wet bag and a banana. "And you have a meet next weekend, so you need the practice. No skipping today."

I groan as I shove everything into my backpack and follow her out to the car to meet Emme.

It actually turns out to be fun. We start with the usual warm-ups and freestyle kicks, but then Emme and Jillian convince Coach Missy to let us play sharks and minnows before the descends.

Once we're back to sprints, Coach Missy picks me to lead my lane. Sometimes when I'm swimming I totally space out. Other times I do math equations or just keep glancing at the clock and counting the minutes until practice is over. But today I start thinking about my mom. My *birth mom*, as Emme would say. I know she was tall, like me, and also had honey-colored hair. She and my dad lived together in Boulder, Colorado. My dad hasn't told me a lot about her, except that she *struggled*. I'm not sure what that means. He also said she didn't have *parenting instincts*, which I think means she didn't want kids. My dad did want kids, though, so he took me and we moved back to Greeley—where he grew up—when I was a baby. He met Margo soon after, and then they got married.

Sometimes I wonder if my birth mom likes sports. Or if she's a worrier like me. I know her name is Christine Tenny. The lawyer told us that the judge might say her name at the adoption hearing. That's the part I'm most nervous about, if the judge says *Christine Tenny* out loud like she's an actual person. Because most of the time it doesn't feel like she is.

After practice, Emme's mom Claire meets us in the lobby. She gives Emme a hug and then hands us both peanut-butter-and-honey sandwiches and milk boxes.

"Eat up," she says. "We have a surprise for you."

"Me?" Emme asks.

"*Both* of you," Claire says.

I raise my eyebrows at Emme, but she shrugs like she's as confused as I am. Ever since Emme switched to Ms. Chung's class last month, she seems much happier. She's said that Gina and the others still give her snotty looks when she passes them in the hall, but at least she doesn't have to be in the same room as them for seven and a half hours every day.

"Can you at least tell us something about the surprise?" Emme asks as we're sliding into the back of the car.

"The thing is," Claire says, "you both have a birthday coming up on New Year's Day. The big eleven."

Emme grins as she buckles her seat belt. "Did you realize it's going to be our first palindrome year?"

"That's so cool!" I say, poking the straw into the milk box. "After that we'll have twenty-two and thirty-three and—"

"Slow down!" Claire says, smiling. "Let's stick with eleven for now."

When we get to Emme's house, we hurry inside and hang our coats on the rack. Julia is washing grapes in the sink. Margo and my dad are sitting on stools at the counter. Margo's belly is getting so big it looks like she has a balloon stuffed under her shirt. I'm almost, sort of, kind of getting used to it. The balloon belly, that is. Not the alien baby.

"What's the surprise?" Emme and I ask at the same time.

Butterball weaves around my legs. I bend over and give him a quick scratch between his ears.

"We've been talking," Julia says as she pours the grapes into a serving bowl.

Margo sips some tea and then says, "And we've decided that you two shouldn't have a birthday party this year."

"Or presents," my dad says, grinning.

"*What?*" I ask. Behind my dad, I can see through the sliding-glass doors. The wind is swirling rusty-brown leaves in circles around the swing set. It's really turning into winter.

"No fair!" Emme says.

"Hang on." My dad points to two envelopes on the counter. "Why don't you check these out first?"

Emme and I dive for the envelopes and tear them open. Inside there are pieces of paper that say:

Emme and Hannah are cordially invited to New York City with Julia and Margo for a moms-and-daughters 11th birthday extravaganza. Fly on an airplane to the Big Apple. Stay in a hotel for two nights. See the Christmas decorations. Visit the Rockefeller Center tree and the Empire State Building. Eat lunch at Peanut Butter & Co.!

> *Love,*
> *Mom J and Mom C*
> *Dad and Margo*

Emme and I stare at each other in shock.

"This is for real?" Emme asks.

Julia nods.

"For really real?" I ask.

Margo wipes at her eyes. "Manhattan isn't a tropical island like we'd talked about, but at least it's an island. And my doctor says I can go."

I set down the paper and hug Margo. And then my dad. And then Emme. And then, just because I'm crazily excited, I hug Julia and Claire. I even scoop up Butterball and nuzzle my nose into his fur. In a way, this is all thanks to Butterball for running away from Emme's house and appearing, wet and shivering, on our side porch. Yes, Sophie moving to Canada felt like the worst thing ever. But it turns out something really amazing came out of it, too.

~~~~~~

On a freezing cold morning in the middle of December, my dad, Margo, and I climb the steps of the Greeley courthouse. I was too nervous to eat breakfast, but now my stomach is rumbling and my toes are pinched in the new brown boots that Margo bought me for the adoption hearing. I'm also wearing a new dark purple dress with a black cardigan. I never wear dresses, but it actually feels right for today.

As soon as we walk into the courtroom, the judge stands up and shakes my parents' hands.

"Hannah?" she asks, holding out her hand to me. "I'm Judge O'Toole. It's so nice to meet you. What a special, important day for you and your family."

I reach out and shake her hand. The lawyer had said that the judge would be a woman, but I pictured her old and wrinkly and scary. Judge O'Toole is wearing a long black robe, but other than that she looks like a regular mom at my school. She's got shiny blond hair, diamond earrings, and a kind smile.

Ryan, our lawyer, is in the courtroom, too. When I met him back in September, he was in jeans, but now he's dressed up in a suit and tie.

"Good morning, Drew and Margo," he says, shaking my parents' hands. He gives me a high five, and then leads us to a long table.

As soon as we sit down, the judge puts on her glasses and clears her throat. That's when everything starts feeling official. I glance around. There's another woman here—she's talking quietly to the judge—and a bald guy and there are even two security guards over by the door.

I'm trying not to think about how they're all here for me.

"The first case on the adoption calendar today," the bald guy says, "is for the matter of Hannah Eileen Strafel."

Okay, it's hard to deny. They *are* all here because of me. My stomach is growling. I wiggle my toes in my boots. I think I'm getting a blister. Margo squeezes my hand.

Judge O'Toole instructs us to go around the table and state our names. As it gets closer to me, my mouth feels dry. What if I can't talk? Or what if I can't remember my name? I wish I could just kick my boots off.

"Hannah?" the judge says. "Can you say your name please?"

I take a deep breath. "Hannah Eileen Strafel."

My dad reaches over and takes my other hand.

"How old are you, Hannah?" asks the woman who was talking to the judge.

"Ten," I say. "I'll be eleven in a couple weeks."

Thinking about that reminds me of how Emme and her mom Julia and Margo and I are going to New York City for our joint birthday. I still can't believe that's happening.

Once everyone has said their names and my dad and Margo give them our address, the judge starts signing papers.

"It's a lot of signing," she says, winking at me. "It'll be a while."

I watch the clock on the far wall. I try not to worry that something is wrong with our paperwork. I've heard that can happen and then you have to wait a few more months for the adoption. Instead I think about how, on the drive to the courthouse, we talked about what I'd call Margo from now on, like if I want to start calling her Mom. I don't know about that. Emme would probably be a good person to ask about it because when we first met she told me how she switched to *Mom C* and *Mom J* when she was eight. Margo said she's fine with anything, but I should know that she's been my mom in every single way since the day she met me. Today is just about making it legal.

"Okay," the judge finally says. "After I sign on this one last line, it's going to be official. Drumroll, please . . ."

The lawyer and the bald guy and the other woman drum on the tabletop with their fingers. I can't help grinning.

"Hannah Eileen Strafel," Judge O'Toole says as she sets down her pen, "you are now officially the daughter of Margo Strafel."

We all start crying and hugging and taking pictures. The judge gives me a gift bag with a gorgeous white picture frame inside.

"To remember this day forever," she says, touching my arm. "Thank you for letting me be a part of it."

As we're walking out of the courtroom, I realize they didn't say Christine Tenny's name after all.

~~~~~

Even though it's only eleven fifteen, my dad, Margo, and I are all so hungry we decide to go to our celebratory lunch early. We drive to an Italian restaurant called Spiga. We went there once before, when Margo finished her master's degree. It's really fancy with white tablecloths and candles and bread-sticks in a basket. I'm about to order penne with Parmesan when I change my mind and say, "I'll get the thin-crust pizza."

"Pizza?" my dad asks.

"Pizza?" Margo asks.

"Pizza," I say.

I kick off my boots under the table and flex my cramped toes. I can't explain why I want to try pizza when I've always insisted it's slithery and gross. Maybe I'm just really hungry. Or maybe things in my life are starting to change.

My dad orders a sausage pizza and Margo and I share a thin-crust veggie supreme. I eat three slices and part of a fourth. I don't know what the opposite of *slithery* is. Scrumptiously yummily perfect? Yes, it's true. The pizza is perfect.

I guess it's been a big day for me in so many ways.

eight

~~~~~~~~~~~~~~~~

EMME

Butterball's new vet is in a low brick building with forest-green trim. The sign out front says KONNING & MORRIS: SMALL ANIMALS, ALL ANIMALS. As Mom J and I pull into the parking lot for my cat's annual checkup, I say, "All animals? Like pandas?"

"Always pandas," Mom J says, smiling. "Who could turn away a panda?"

We're both in a great mood because we're going on a road trip tomorrow afternoon. We're driving to Connecticut to see my cousin, Leesa, play ukulele in a holiday concert at her boarding school. My aunt and uncle, Leesa's parents, live down in South Carolina, so we'll be her only family members there. We're going to leave right after school on Friday, drive partway, and sleep in a hotel. On Saturday, we'll take Leesa out to lunch and then see her concert that evening. At some point, maybe at lunch, I want to tell Leesa about how the collage got ruined. My moms say I don't have to. I can just say I lost it and we need to start another one. They say it's not really a lie—more like I'm protecting myself from feeling bad all over again.

I lug Butterball's travel case with me out of the backseat. He's cowered in one corner, ears flat, looking nervous. He's wearing Hannah's blue collar today. Between Butterball and the carrying case, the whole thing weighs so much I can barely make it across the parking lot.

"Can you take him?" I huff, passing the case over to Mom J.

"Oh, you fat, fat cat." Mom J peers into the gate door. "Your judgment day is here."

Sure enough, the vet comes down hard on Butterball. After Dr. Konning flips through his chart and gives him his shots, she crosses her arms over her chest and says, "I know you've heard this before, but—"

"He needs to lose weight?" I ask.

The vet scratches Butterball's head and says, "This sweetie? Big-time."

Dr. Konning has long dark hair, chocolate-brown eyes, and an accent. When I ask where she's from, she says the

Netherlands. I can tell she loves cats by the way she keeps nuzzling Butterball and saying what a sweetie he is.

"According to your last vet in Florida," she says, "Butterball weighed eleven pounds. Now he's thirteen."

"That much?" Mom J asks.

"It's all the Oceanfish and Tuna," I say, wrinkling my nose.

"Well, things need to change," the vet says. "He's a six-year-old overweight male cat and—"

"We *think* he's six," I say. "He was a stray."

Dr. Konning nods. "If he doesn't lose weight, he's at high risk of getting diabetes or arthritis or other serious diseases."

Dr. Konning prints out paperwork on feline diets and explains how we need to switch his food and buy chasing toys to get him exercise. All the while, Butterball purrs and nuzzles into the vet's fingers. He has no clue he's about to start kitty boot camp.

Back in the car, Mom J and I are quiet. I guess we noticed that Butterball was plumping up but we didn't realize it was such a big deal. Before we go home, Mom J wants to swing by the pet store to get diet cat food to bring to Hannah's house. Her family is going to watch Butterball while we're away this weekend.

"I can't imagine Butterball getting a disease," I say, fiddling with the zipper on my new parka.

Mom J glances at the travel case next to me on the backseat. "We'll help him lose weight. He just has to stop sneaking food. Are you okay, Em? Your cheeks are flushed."

I roll my eyes. "I'm fine. I've got my winter coat on. I'm not sick. I can go to school tomorrow. Who's he sneaking food from?"

"Up and down Centennial. Some neighbors have told me he comes begging for treats. Speaking of you staying home sick, I've been meaning to tell you about—"

"Naughty cat!" I say, tapping his case. He's licking his paw, still oblivious. "*Butterball* is totally the wrong name for a cat on a diet. Remember how Hannah named him Radar that time he ran away? Maybe that'd be better for him."

As we pull into the pet store, I realize I never did get to hear what Mom J was going to say before about me being sick. Because I'm not sick. Huh.

~~~~~

That night, my moms and I carry Butterball and all his gear over to Hannah's house. We've got his dish, his water bowl, his diet food, his litter box, extra litter, his new laser pen and string toys to chase, and a scratching post so he doesn't mutilate their couch. Hannah's sitting at the kitchen table, eating a slice of cold pizza piled with vegetables.

"*Pizza?*" I ask. This is as shocking as if I walked in on Hannah eating worms. "What on earth are you doing?"

Hannah shrugs. "I had some at a restaurant yesterday and it was so good. Want a slice? We have leftovers. Sausage, too."

I shake my head quickly and step backward. Even *looking* at pizza grosses me out, the way the yellowish cheese and red sauce blend together and get all pink and gloppy. Hannah has always said the same thing. We've always said we're the only kids in America who hate pizza.

"So what if Butterball asks for food and he's already had his meal?" Hannah asks, wiping her mouth with a napkin. "He nips at your ankles, right?"

Butterball is sniffing around under the table. I hoist him into my arms. I still can't look at the pizza on Hannah's plate. I still can't believe she's eating it. "If he's begging for food, you should distract him. You can shine that laser beam onto the wall and get him to chase it around."

"I heard there's an app where a cat can chase mice on the screen," she says.

"Seriously?"

Hannah nods and then calls into the living room. "Margo? Dad? Does Butterball using the iPad count as my screen time?"

All the parents are in the living room admiring a massive collection of baby gear that's been accumulating by their window—a car seat, a stroller, a stack of folded blankets, a giraffe mobile, even a portable crib. I've noticed items arriving over the past few weeks, but Hannah never says a word about them.

"Yes, it counts!" Margo calls into the kitchen.

"You too, Emme," Mom C says. "Butterball's screen time is your screen time."

Hannah grins and flips her hair over her shoulder. "It was worth a try."

In the center of the table, they have the vase with the flowers we brought over last night, as an adoption gift. It's a ceramic vase filled with red tulips. According to my moms' bulb book (yep, they're still obsessed with bulbs), red tulips symbolize eternal love.

"Your hair's getting so long," I say. I recently got my hair cut to my chin, like a blunt bob. When I met Hannah in August we had the same hairstyle.

"I know," Hannah says. "I can finally put it all up in a ponytail. I'm going to grow it way down my back."

In my head, I'm thinking, *She's eating pizza . . . She's growing her hair out . . . What's happening to the Og Twins?* But instead I say, "Cool." Because we still have swimming. And palindromes. And our joint birthday. And our trip to New York City.

Just like an Og Twin, Hannah reads my last thought. "Can you believe we're going to New York City in two weeks?"

"I was thinking the same thing," I say. "We should go ice-skating in Central Park. Wouldn't that be awesome?"

Hannah frowns. "Maybe."

Before I can ask what's wrong, Mom J says it's time to go home and pack for our road trip.

~~~~~

At school the next day, Ms. Chung announces that we're doing an anti-bullying workshop instead of gym.

"Every fifth-grade class will have three workshops on this important topic," Ms. Chung says, smoothing the silk scarf around her neck. That's how she talks (sort of formal).

I look to see if anyone is staring at me (they're not). Even so, my cheeks are heating up. I wonder if they're doing these workshops because of what happened to me in Ms. Linhart's class. I know my moms had a meeting with the principal about making sure they have zero tolerance for bullying at Greeley Elementary.

I walk down to the gym with Jillian. She swims in the silver level with Hannah and me. She reminds me of my friend Olivia from Captiva Island. Not a best friend, but a good person to hang out with. Honestly, everyone in Ms. Chung's class is nice. Ms. Chung is older, with threads of white in her black hair, and the whole classroom vibe (as Leesa would say) is calm. It's not a constant party like Mr. Bryce's class, but it's *so, so, so* much better than Ms. Linhart's. Whenever I see Gina or Haley or Alexa in the cafeteria, I get shaky all over. Usually I stare at my lunch until they pass by. I don't want to make eye contact with them or hear them say "O.M.G.!" or give them any chance to dis me.

When we get to the gym there's a super-tall African American guy with a goatee giving everyone high fives. He must be at least six foot six.

"My name's Tim Mitchell," he tells us as we gather around him on the polished wooden floor, "but people call me Tiny. Get it? Because I'm tiny."

We all laugh. It *is* funny to think that his nickname is Tiny. He's so tall that he'd make Mom C look short.

"Sometimes you have to embrace the joke," Tiny says, walking back and forth in front of us. Then he stops and his face gets serious. "And sometimes you don't. Sometimes people cross lines that they shouldn't cross or that you don't want them to cross. That's what we're here to talk about."

Tiny starts by saying how most of us have probably been bullied at some point, and it's nothing to be ashamed about. In fact, there's a lot we can learn from the experience.

"But I'm not going to start with the bully," he says. "I'm going to start with the bystanders. You know them, right? The people on the sidelines grinning and fueling the fire, or even just watching and not doing anything?"

I immediately think about the other kids in Ms. Linhart's class and how they were whispering and laughing when someone (probably Gina, Alexa, or Haley) wrote *LOSER* on my collage.

"The thing is," Tiny says, "if you don't have bystanders, the bully doesn't have much to keep him or her going. No reaction."

Tiny uncaps a marker, walks over to a big pad of paper, and has us brainstorm ways to be actively involved protectors instead of not-so-innocent bystanders. We're all calling out stuff like "Walk away!" "Get a teacher!" "Tell the bully to quit it!" Then some kids tell Tiny how they've been bullied. Jillian says it happened to her in second grade. I have to wonder if Gina and her friends were involved.

Tiny sets down his marker. "Now we're going to move around a little. We're going to do something called the Mookey Line."

We all stare at him.

"Who's ever heard of *mookey*?"

Again, silence.

"Good," Tiny says, "because it's a made-up word. But let's pretend it's an insult. A really bad one. I'm going to have you guys stand in two lines, facing each other." When no one moves, Tiny says, "Come on, let's do it!"

We all hustle into two lines. I'm next to Jillian and a guy with a cast on one arm. His name is Leo.

"Okay, I'm going to walk down the center of you guys and you all need to shout *mookey* at me. Really let me have it . . . and watch what I do."

Tiny walks in the aisle between us and we all start saying *mookey* to him. At first we're low-key about it, but after a second we're belting it out. "Mookey!" we scream.

"Mookey! Mookey!" Some kids even jab their fingers toward him.

The thing is, Tiny never once looks at us. He just walks along, eyes forward, shoulders back.

"And that is how you walk the Mookey Line," he says, holding up his hand to silence us. "You keep your head up and you don't let them get to you. You don't give them a reaction. Who wants to go next?"

I have no idea how it happens but my hand shoots into the air.

"Brave soul," Tiny says, smiling down at me. He must be twice my height. "Come on over here. What's your name?"

"Emme."

"Emme." He gestures toward my class, still in parallel lines. "Walk the Mookey Line."

I take my first step and everyone starts shouting at me. I thought it would be scary, but it actually feels cool to hold my head high and ignore them all.

Leo goes next, and then a few other guys, and then Jillian. By the end, we've all had a turn to walk the Mookey Line.

As we leave the gym, our class passes Ms. Linhart's class lined up outside for their workshop. When I see Gina (standing apart from Haley and Alexa?!?), I look her right in the eye. She looks back at me for a second, and then she turns away.

~~~~~

My moms pick me up right after school and we leave for Connecticut. Mom C took the afternoon off and they loaded the car with chips and peanut butter cookies and trail mix. We drive until it's dark, and then eat dinner and sleep over in a hotel.

We arrive in eastern Connecticut around lunchtime the next day. Leesa's boarding school is surrounded by a low stone fence. Inside are brick buildings, statues, and acres of fields and trees. It's amazing to think she lives here. It looks like something from a movie.

We call Leesa and make a plan to meet her in front of her dorm. When we pull up, she skips toward our car, waving wildly. Her hair is arranged in about fifteen braids with ribbon strung through them. She's wearing a black coat, checkered tights, and tall magenta boots. I haven't seen her in a year, but she looks as good-vibey as ever.

"Aunt Claire! Aunt Julia! Emme!" Leesa says, hugging all of us.

It's bitter cold out, so we quickly pile back into the car.

Leesa is in the backseat next to me. We drive across campus to the main office. As my moms go inside to sign Leesa out, my cousin squeezes my arm. "You're still so teeny, cuz. It's really cute."

Teeny and *cute* make me sound like a baby chick. "I've grown a little," I say. (Okay, a half inch in the past six months, but I'll take it.)

My moms return to the car and we pull through the front gate. We're going to a restaurant for lunch (French food, Leesa's choice).

Leesa sings to herself on the drive. "It's a song from the concert tonight," she says to me. "I'll be playing this on my ukulele."

"Cool," I say.

After a few minutes, we get stuck behind a slow-moving vehicle. I decide to get my (semi-true) confession out of the way now so I can enjoy the rest of lunch. I lean over to Leesa. "You know how you sent the collage back to me a while ago?"

Leesa grins. "Did you like the gas thingy? Awesome, right? Someone in my dorm gave me that picture."

I nod. "I loved it, except . . ." I pause. A white lie is okay. It wasn't my fault the collage got ruined. "I, uh, lost it. Is it okay if we start another one? I can mail you the first installment."

Leesa shrugs. "No biggie. *Actch*, let's chill on the collages for now. I'm kind of over it."

I stare at Leesa. I thought she might be mad that I said I lost the collage. The last thing I expected was that she wanted to quit doing them.

"No offense," she says. "I'm just busy with school and all."

"That's fine," I say quietly, even though it sort of isn't.

The restaurant is called Delphine's. From the second we sit down until when the food arrives, Leesa talks about herself and her friends and the concert tonight and what she's doing over winter break. *Actch*, it's a little annoying. I have so much I want to tell her about Greeley and Hannah and our new house and swim team and switching classrooms. But whenever I try to talk, she interrupts me with a story about herself. After a while, I focus on my hamburger and fries. They brought three kinds of dip (ketchup, mayonnaise, and garlic oil), so I'm alternating one fry per dip.

Finally, the waiter brings out the dessert menus. Mom J and Mom C can never decide what to get for dessert so they always order two and share them. I'm getting chocolate ice cream. Leesa tells me she's going to order a platter of cheese.

"Cheese?" I ask.

"That's what they do in France," she says.

She pronounces it the French way, *Frawnce*. I want to tell her we're not *in Frawnce*, but I don't say anything.

"So where are you staying?" Leesa asks, touching a ribbon woven into one of her braids.

Mom J tells her the name of the hotel. It's a few miles from the boarding school.

"Coolio," Leesa says, turning to me. "Do you still sleep with that gnarly old rabbit?"

I stare at my cousin. "Bun-Bun?" I've slept with Bun-Bun since I was a baby. No big deal. Mom C says she brought her stuffed harp seal to *college* with her.

"That's *sooo* cute," Leesa says. "Probably time for good-bye to Bun-Bun, though. Time for the big-girl bed."

I'm not sure if my moms heard that because they're still debating fruit tart versus custard versus mousse. I ask Leesa if she has a boyfriend but she rolls her eyes and says people don't do that at her school. Leesa turns one of her many earrings. I'm starting to wonder if looking like you have good vibes and *having* good vibes are two separate things.

"By the way, Aunt Julia," Leesa says to Mom J after we've ordered our dessert, "congrats on the article. My dad sent me a link."

"Oh," Mom J says, her eyes widening. "Thank you."

"What article?" I ask.

Mom J looks over at Mom C, who nods encouragingly. And just like that, I know what Mom J is going to say. She wrote another "Potty-Training Emme and Other Disasters," fifth-grade edition.

"Did you write about me?" I ask quickly.

Mom J winces. "I tried to tell you a few days ago, but—"

"What was the article about?" I twist my napkin in my hands.

"The three-o'clock miracle," Mom J says in a false attempt at brightness. "I wrote about it for a parenting website, about what to do if your child comes home sick but then feels better at—"

"You wrote about *that*?" I hiss. "You wrote about what happened to me at school? Did you use my name?"

"Of course not," Mom J says, shaking her head. "I just said *my daughter*."

"But we have the same last name," I say.

"The Hoffman part, yes."

"I actually think it's cute. When I was—" Leesa starts to say, but now it's my turn to cut her off.

"It's NOT cute," I say to Leesa. Then I turn to Mom J. "Please don't write about me anymore without my permission."

The waiter delivers the desserts. He must sense a chill around the table because he sets everything down and scurries off.

"Be respectful to your mom," Mom C says in her serious lawyer voice.

Well, I'm not going to let that intimidate me, either. Because this is another Mookey Line. Except I'm realizing that sometimes I should keep my head high and let it all wash over me. And sometimes I have to face it. That's what I'm going to say the next time Tiny comes in for a workshop. There's more than one way to walk the Mookey Line.

I sit up as tall as possible (not saying much, but at least I'm taller than a baby chicken) and say, "Mom J needs to respect my life, too. It's mine. I'm not material for articles. Also"—I turn to Leesa—"I'm almost eleven. I'm not cute. And I'm not teeny."

As everyone stares at me, I pick up my spoon and start eating my chocolate ice cream.

nine

~~~~~~~~~~

HANNAH

The good news is that today is the Friday before winter break. Twelve days off from school. My eleventh birthday. A trip to New York City with my best friend.

The bad news is, well, everything else.

For one, we have a swim meet tomorrow—the all-county semifinals—that'll take up the entire day. I'm so sick of the competition and timed trials and endless practices. And meets like these go on FOREVER.

For two, my dad cleared out the guest room and painted it blue. He and Margo are calling it pajama blue, but the truth is that it's totally baby blue. Now they're arranging it with all the baby gear that had been piling up in the living room. The fact that there's *baby* furniture in a *baby*-blue room is making the alien baby a lot harder to deny.

For three, I can't stand how everyone gets obsessed with ice-skating in the winter. Even Emme, who's from *Florida*, keeps talking about ice-skating. I tried it once a few years ago, fell straight backward, and nearly cracked my cranium. Who ever thought of racing across ice with *knives* attached to boots? The thing is, I'm worried if I tell people that I'm scared of skating they'll think I'm lame.

Oh, and for four, the weather forecast is bad. No, not bad. Terrible.

The weather people are predicting massive amounts of snow in the next week or two. They're warning that holiday travel could be majorly messed up.

We're at morning meeting and I'm going to share about my trip to New York City. But first Mr. Bryce tells us he has an exciting announcement.

"We received a letter from the mayor of Deer Park thanking us for our contribution to the flood recovery effort," Mr. Bruce says, holding up a piece of paper. "They earmarked our funds for elementary school kids whose families lost their homes, and everyone is incredibly grateful. I've made copies for the class." Mr. Bryce picks up a stack of letters off his desk. "Denny? Marley? Can you help me pass these out?"

I reach out and take my letter from Denny. Ever since the fight at the apple-cider stand, things have settled down between the boys and the girls. Mr. Bryce was upset about our warfare in the park, but he also said that he made a mistake by pitting us against each other. I was impressed that he admitted to messing up. Teachers don't usually do that.

"Okay, Hannah," Mr. Bryce says, nodding to me. He's wearing a snowman tie today. "I know you had something to share with the class."

I fold the Deer Park letter in half and tuck it in my notebook. "I'm going on a trip to New York City over break," I say. "For my eleventh birthday. I'm going with my friend Emme, and we're going to see the tree at Rockefeller Center and the store windows and the Empire State Building. Over the holidays, they light it up green and red."

"That's awesome!" Max says.

"I know," I say, grinning. "I can't believe it."

But I will believe it. Even with all the forecasts about a blizzard coming.

Layla leans in and whispers to me, "Can you get me a snow globe with a New York City scene? I collect them. I'll pay you back."

"Sure," I say, nodding. "Definitely."

The next day, my dad and Margo go to a seven-hour child-birth class—*not thinking about it, not thinking about it*—so Emme's mom Julia takes us to the swim meet. Once Emme and I have changed into our racing suits, we sit next to each other on the pool deck and uncap our Sharpies. I write *Go Emme Og* down one leg and *Eat My Bubbles* on the other leg. As I record my heats and lanes on my arm, my stomach scrambles nervously. I wish it was hours from now and the semifinals were over.

When Emme goes to fill up her water bottle, I find Coach Missy sitting on the bleachers, studying her clipboard. She has on her mismatched white and blue flip-flops, and she's wearing a Santa Claus hat that says *Coach* in glitter on the front.

"What's up, Og Twin?" Coach Missy asks me.

"I brought you this," I say, sitting next to her and handing her the letter from the mayor of Deer Park. "We got it from school yesterday."

Coach Missy reads the letter. "That's so sweet," she says. "I'll tell my sister about it. She's already back in her home, just some minor repairs from the flood damage."

I move my straps around on my shoulders. My racing suit is so tight it leaves red grooves on my skin. I *really* don't want to be up on the blocks, diving into the water, when they sound the buzzer. Whenever I imagine myself up there, I feel like hiding in the locker room and never coming out.

"You're not feeling it today, are you?" Coach Missy asks.

I shrug. "Not really."

"Are you sick?"

I shake my head.

"Hannah," Coach Missy says, "I know you've been iffy about swimming recently. I'm sure you and your parents are talking about it, and I trust you'll make the right choice. From my perspective, you're a tall, strong, athletic girl, and you're on your way to being a very talented swimmer. You already are."

"But what if I took a break?" I say to Coach Missy. It feels weird to say it out loud. I actually haven't talked about it with my parents yet. Sometimes it feels like they're too consumed by the alien baby to think about anything else.

"Of course that's an option," she says, "but it's always harder to come back to swimming once you're out."

Just then, Emme skips over. "What's up?" she asks, sipping from her water bottle.

"Nothing," I say quickly. I'm worried Emme will be mad if I drop out of swimming, like she'll think I don't want to be friends anymore. Which is *so* not true.

"Just some nerves," Coach Missy says, touching my arm.

I push myself off the bleachers and Emme and I join the rest of our team on the deck.

~~~~~

The first part of Christmas break goes by fast. We exchange presents. We have Uncle Peter over for Christmas dinner. We watch movies. Emme and I bake peanut butter cookies, both of our first times using the oven without an adult. The next day, Emme invites me to go ice-skating at an indoor rink near the mall. I didn't want to tell her I was scared of skating so I was glad I had a built-in excuse. I already had plans to go to Layla's house. Layla has a ping-pong table, unlimited screen time, and a stash of candy in her pantry.

Some evenings, Emme and I take Butterball galloping up and down her stairs, chasing catnip mice and laser beams. Emme says he's losing weight, but he's so lumpy it's hard to tell. One time, when Margo and my dad are at work, I peek into the baby's room. It's actually sweet, with a yellow rocking chair and a giraffe mobile over the crib and the faintest whiff of baby powder. Of course, it's currently empty. Ask me how I feel about the room when the alien is living here.

My birthday is now two days away. It hasn't snowed yet, not one little flake, but the weather people are still predicting that a major blizzard is coming.

"I can't wait to see real snow," Emme says on the phone. "I've never seen snow in my entire life."

I sit on a chair in the kitchen and twirl a pen in my fingers. "I find that hard to believe. How can someone have *never* seen snow?"

"I'm from Florida, remember?" Emme says. "We've been up north in the spring before, and in the fall, too. Like, to Boston and a few other places. But most people from Florida don't go where it's *cold* in the winter."

"Just so you know," I say, clicking and unclicking the pen, "blizzards shut down airports. Blizzards ruin entire trips."

Emme groans. "So I'll hope for snow once we get back from New York City, and then for every single day after that."

Later that day, I plan my New York City outfits. We're flying on January 1 and sleeping over for two nights. One of those evenings we'll be going to a fancy restaurant. I'm packing the purple dress that I wore to my adoption hearing, and I've been working hard to break in my brown boots. For the other dinner out in New York City, I'll wear leggings and a sweater.

The morning before the trip, I grab my dad's phone and check out the forecast.

"Fifty percent chance of a major snowstorm," I say, looking up from the screen. It's New Year's Eve day, the day before our birthday. Emme and I are in the kitchen, eating the last of our homemade cookies.

Emme's an optimist, so of course she says, "That's fifty percent we're going."

"Or fifty percent we're not."

"Let's hope we're going," Emme says. "Glass half full."

Margo's being an optimist, too. She and Julia keep texting each other, and they both check in for our flight, which is at ten tomorrow morning. That afternoon, Margo pulls the suitcases out of the hall closet and helps me pack my clothes. For Christmas she gave me a polka-dot toiletries bag with travel-size shampoo and toothpaste and a toothbrush that folds into a little lid.

"Do you *really* think the trip is going to happen?" I ask, tucking an extra pair of wool socks into my suitcase. Supposedly we have to be ready to walk everywhere in New York City, even when it's cold.

Margo and I glance out the window. It's snowing lightly, little swirls of powder on our front lawn.

"The forecast isn't great," Margo says, sighing heavily, "but you never know. The storm could pass right over us."

Margo sighs again. She sighs all the time now. She said it's because the baby is getting so big there's not much room for her lungs in there. Nice kid.

I go to bed around ten, but then wake up at midnight because everyone on Centennial Avenue is shouting "Happy New Year!" and honking their horns. I sit up and look out my window.

It's snowing so hard I can barely see anything. So much for glass half full.

~~~~~

I wake up early on my birthday—like, before six.

I don't think: *I'm eleven!*

I don't think: *It's a new year!*

All I think is: *Are we going to New York City?*

I hear Margo down in the kitchen. Supposedly the baby kicks so much that she can hardly sleep. As I said, nice kid.

On my way down the stairs, I try not to look out the front window, but I can't help it. The snowdrifts are so high I can't see our driveway. And even though I hear the scraping of snowplows in the distance, they haven't made it to Centennial Avenue yet. In fact, where is our street? All I can see in the early-morning light is snow.

"Hey, honey," Margo says as I walk into the kitchen. She's sitting in a bathrobe at the table, eating a ham sandwich and drinking a glass of milk. Being pregnant makes her have weird cravings. "Happy birthday and happy New Year."

"The airport's closed, isn't it?" I ask.

"Yep," Margo says, nodding. "They don't think flights will be going out until tomorrow or even the day after."

"So the trip is canceled? Definitely?"

Margo rests one hand on her belly. "Unfortunately yes. I'm so sorry, Hannah. We knew this was a possibility, but—"

"Can we do it another weekend? Like, can we reschedule?"

"The problem is, I'm thirty-three weeks pregnant. I was pushing it to take this trip. By next week, my doctor doesn't want me flying."

I stare at my stepmom. I mean, my mom. "So that's *it*? It's just over?"

"We'll figure something out," Margo says.

I turn on my slipper and walk back up to my room. I'm not trying to be a brat, but when adults say they'll *figure something out*, it generally means things are getting downgraded in a major way.

I've been looking forward to my first palindrome year since forever. And now it's turning into one big zero.

~~~~~

My parents had said that New York City was my birthday gift, but it turns out they got me some other presents, too. They give me four headbands, three books, a gift certificate to Sports Authority, and a new volleyball. Also, Sophie sent me a card with cats singing "Happy Birthday" and a bracelet that says *Ottawa*. That's the city she moved to in Canada. My dad makes hash browns for breakfast and Margo blends my chocolate milk so it's frothy. I'm trying to be grateful, but I'm still feeling lousy. After breakfast, I go back up to my room.

Around nine, Emme knocks on my bedroom door.

"Happy birthday, Og Twin!" she sings. She's taken off her boots but she's still wearing her parka and hat. "I'm seriously freaking out about the snow! It's just so white. I know it stinks that our trip is postponed, but it's snowing! Want to go sledding?"

"Happy birthday, too," I say, flopping onto my bed. "You sound so happy. Don't you care about the trip? And it's not postponed, at least for me. It's canceled."

"I was thinking we could make the best of it though," Emme says. "My moms don't want to take me to the ice rink because the roads are bad and they're worried about driving in so much snow, but we could walk to a sledding hill. I've never been sledding. Well, duh, of course I haven't! You know a good hill, right?"

"I don't want to go sledding," I say gruffly. I mean, *come on*! She's acting like it's any old fun snow day. "And the truth is, I can't stand ice-skating, so I don't feel like doing that, either."

"Okay." Emme bites her bottom lip. "Well . . . happy birthday."

As Emme walks down the stairs, I roll over on my bed.

My zero birthday just dipped into the negative numbers. Exactly like the temperature outside.

~~~~

I spend the morning in my room. I read a few chapters of a new book. I arrange the photos on my dresser—Sophie and me, Emme and me, and one of my dad, Margo, and me in the white frame that the judge gave me. I try on my headbands. I get the iPad and look up images of New York City at Christmastime.

I can hear Emme and Claire and Julia in their backyard. I think my dad's out there with them. I feel bad I was so grumpy with Emme. She was just excited about seeing snow for the first time. And it's her birthday, too, after all. Her trip was canceled just like mine.

I click on a picture of the ice-skating rink at Rockefeller Center and suddenly I get a crazy idea.

"Margo?" I ask, running down to the kitchen. "Can I do something?"

She's got a few jars of peanut butter on the counter, several flavors of jam, and a loaf of bread. She spins around quickly and tosses a dish towel over the peanut butter.

"Hey, birthday girl," she says. "Are you feeling better? And can you be more specific about what you want to do?"

"The thing is," I say, "I was wondering if I could get out our garden hose and spray water all over the backyard to make it into an ice-skating rink."

Margo stares at me. "You want to do that for Emme?"

"Can I?"

She rinses her hands in the sink. "I want to show you something. Put on your coat and boots and come on outside. Grab your hat and gloves, too. The temperature is dropping."

Margo and I head out the side door. Sure enough, Emme and her moms and my dad are in her backyard. When they see me, Emme runs over. Her cheeks are bright red and her hat is covered in snow.

"Look!" she says, gesturing behind her. "We're bringing New York City to you."

I look into her yard and suck in my breath even though my lungs are icy from the bitter cold. They've built a snowman that looks like the Statue of Liberty, complete with a crown and a small orange shovel for a torch. They've strung white lights around a pine tree, and my dad and Julia are wrapping red and green lights around the swing set.

"That's the Rockefeller Center tree," Emme says, pointing at the pine tree, "and the swing set will be the Empire State Building. See how we put that stick on top for the point?"

I can't stop smiling. I was going to make an ice rink for Emme, and she's made New York City for me. They all have.

"I love it," I say, hugging Emme. Her parka is so puffy she feels like a human sleeping bag.

Emme wipes at her nose with her glove. "I'm glad."

"I'm sorry about before," I say. "I was disappointed about the trip and—"

"We're the Og Twins," she says. "It's okay. Besides, I thought of a really good palindrome. Want to hear it? *Won snow.* Isn't that awesome?"

"Won snow," I say, nodding. "If there's anything we won today, it's definitely snow."

I pull my fleece hat out of my pocket, tug it over my ears, and tell Emme about the ice rink idea. We get to work immediately, uncoiling the hose from the garage and spraying my yard with water. My dad says he'll research backyard rinks, but we figure we may as well get started with the water because it'll take a while to freeze. Actually, it's so cold it probably won't even take that long. It might even be frozen by tomorrow morning.

~~~~~

After we've sprayed water on a good portion of my backyard, my fingers are so cold I can hardly bend them. Margo invites everyone inside for lunch and hot cocoa. It's a total surprise when she serves us sandwiches with peanut butter. Well, not the sandwich part. It's the peanut butter— maple, white chocolate, and cinnamon raisin. She ordered them as a present from that peanut-butter restaurant in New York City!

As we gather around our table—me and my parents, Emme and her parents—eating sandwiches and drinking mugs of cocoa, I realize it's becoming a great birthday.

"Thanks, you guys," I say, "for, you know, everything."

"Are you having a glass-half-full moment?" Emme asks, biting into her second sandwich. This one is maple peanut butter with Nutella.

I swirl my mini-marshmallows around in the hot chocolate. "More like *mug* half full."

We both laugh. Because it is a mug-half-full day. Definitely.

~~~

Later that evening, Emme and I are stretched out in my living room watching a movie. We've opened the couch so it's a bed, and piled it with pillows. We're having a sleepover, and my parents said we can stay up late and have as much screen time as we want.

We pause the movie for a snack break and head into the kitchen. I look out the back window. It's dark, but I can see by the yard lights that the snow is still coming down.

"Do you think it's frozen yet?" I ask Emme.

"The rink? Maybe. It's so cold out."

"Want to check?"

Emme tosses back a handful of cheese popcorn. "Totally! My skates are in my garage. I'll run over and grab them and you can get yours and we'll meet in the backyard."

I don't own ice skates. *Obviously*, I don't own ice skates. Somehow I didn't consider the fact that making an ice rink means I have to try skating again. Duh.

"If you don't have skates," Emme says, "we can always take turns with mine. They might be a little small on you, but—"

"Do you think it's completely lame if I slide around on boots?" I ask. Even the prospect of being on ice in *boots* makes me nervous, but I'll do it for Emme. Especially after she created a backyard New York City for me. And forgave me for this morning.

Emme shrugs. "Whatever. You can always trade with me if you want."

Five minutes later, Emme and I meet in my backyard. We both have our coats and hats and gloves on, but she's clomping in her ice skates. She looks so much taller with her skates on, even taller than me.

Emme and I lean down and rap our knuckles against the frozen puddles of ice. From what I can see with the light from the porch, the water has frozen in various icy patches throughout the yard.

"I guess it's not like a real ice rink," I say to Emme.

Emme is grinning as she leans over to tighten her skates. "I've never been to an outdoor rink before. This is a perfect first time."

Emme steps onto the ice and then reaches back for me. My heart is pounding and my teeth are chattering. I carefully inch forward. It's slippery, but I don't fall backward and smash my skull like the last time I was on the ice.

As we make our way slowly around my yard, holding hands and slipping from frozen puddle to frozen puddle, Emme says, "I know we're not in New York City, but I still love it."

"What do you mean we're not in New York City?" I use my free hand to point to her backyard, to the swing set dressed in red and green lights and the lit-up pine tree and the snowman with the shovel-torch. "That's the Empire State Building over there. And the Statue of Liberty." I gesture all around me. "And if that's the famous Christmas tree, then this is the Rockefeller Center ice rink."

Emme giggles. "It's amazing, right? We have Rockefeller Center all to ourselves." Then she tips her face to the sky and shouts, "I love New York!"

"Me too," I say, laughing. "I love New York!"

Emme starts singing "New York, New York," except she doesn't know most of the words and neither do I. But we still attempt to sing it as we slip around the backyard, the sky hazy with snow, my best friend and me.

ten

EMME

"Emme?" Mom J says as she stands in our doorway, car keys in her hand. "You're really okay being home alone? Remember to practice calling me from the landline. And Margo is right next door if you need anything."

It's a chilly, gray day in the middle of January. Hannah calls this the dog days of winter. I'm paler than I've ever been. Even my freckles are pale. I'm sprawled on the rug, my pencils all around me. I'm trying to finish a self-portrait that I started in art club but I'm so distracted I keep messing up and making my nose crooked. Mom J is headed to her first day as a volunteer at a greenhouse-gardening program for children. She and Mom C came up with this idea after I got upset about her three-o'clock-miracle story. At the greenhouse, Mom J can spend time with other kids, get new ideas for articles, and not always write about me. Also, she says she wants to meet more friends in Greeley. *Friends.* That's what's on my mind, too, right now.

"Emme? Did you hear me?"

I shade in under one eyebrow. It's not like this is the first time I've been home alone. "Yeah, that's fine."

"You'll feed Butterball his diet food at five? And put more water in his dish? I think he's finished his water already."

"Yep," I say, grabbing my eraser.

"If you can get your homework done," Mom J says, "let's go to the ice rink after dinner."

"Really?" I ask, looking up.

Mom J nods. "Do you think Hannah would want to come?"

I shake my head glumly. No, I'm not just thinking about *friends.* I'm thinking about Hannah.

"Probably not," I say.

"Why not? Wasn't she going to give it another try?"

Her backyard rink ended up being fun, especially that first night. It's not like it was real skating, but we did get some decent strides in, even with Hannah wearing her snow boots. After our homemade rink, Hannah said she'd try real ice-skating with me. But whenever I ask her to go, she's always running off to play volleyball at the Y or shooting hoops in the freezing cold.

"You should probably go to your gardening thing," I say to Mom J. "It's after four."

Mom J hurries out the front door, locking it behind her.

Once she's gone, I crumple up my self-portrait and grab a new sheet of paper. I'm totally messing up today. I'm just so worried. Usually, Hannah is the official worrier of the Og Twins, but something has been bothering me these past few weeks: I think Hannah is going to drop out of the Dolphins. She hasn't said anything to me, but she keeps skipping practices and when she *does* come swimming I often see her whispering with Coach Missy on the bench.

I'm worried that if Hannah stops swimming and starts playing *whatever*ball she'll get to be best friends with the sporty girls and they'll swing their long hair around and eat pizza together every day.

And then it will be the end of the Og Twins.

~~~~~

Sure enough, on the way to practice the next day, Hannah is saying how the last thing she wants to do is swim laps for two hours. It's actually only an hour and forty-five minutes, but I'm not going to tell her that.

I'm eating my banana and looking out the window when Hannah leans forward toward Margo. "Do I really, really have to swim today?"

I can see in the rearview mirror that Margo is frowning. "Let's just get through today. That's what we talked about."

What we talked about. The banana feels thick in my mouth.

Hannah groans and peels back the wrapper on her fruit leather. "I wish I could skip it."

I rub my stomach, but it keeps flipping like crazy.

But then, when we get to the locker room, Hannah is acting normal again.

"Guess what?" she says as we're hanging our coats in the lockers. "My dad is picking us up and bringing cupcakes. Vanilla with dark-chocolate frosting."

"Yum," I say. My throat is hurting a little, but it's hard to say no to a cupcake.

Hannah nods. "Only the best for the Og Twins."

Og Twins. She said it (I'm counting that as a good thing).

We change into our swimsuits. We have matching practice suits, black Speedos with splashes of yellow, bright green, and white. We both have blue Dolphins swim caps. Hannah's says STRAFEL on the front. My last name (Hoffman-Shields) is wrapped around the circumference of my head.

As I pull my cap on and we head to the pool, Hannah links elbows with me. "Whoever thought of hyphenated last names," she says, "never saw a team swim cap."

So true. I have to laugh. (Another good thing.)

But then, as we're doing our butterfly laps, Hannah hoists herself out of the pool and starts talking to Coach Missy again. Coach Missy is nodding and her face looks serious. I also notice that Hannah's toenails aren't painted anymore. Mine are currently black-and-white-striped.

I'm so focused on watching Hannah and Coach Missy that I lose my rhythm, swim too fast, and smash into Jillian's legs. The kid behind me slams into me and it's one big traffic pileup. I end up getting a gush of chlorine up my nostrils. Which also stinks. Literally.

～～～～

That night, I'm on the stairs giving Butterball his nightly exercise. It's not that hard. I just pull a catnip mouse on a string and he pounces after it. Whatever we're doing seems to be working. We put him on my moms' scale the other day and he's already down to eleven and a half pounds. Dr. Konning is going to be so impressed when we bring him back.

"Emme?" Mom C calls from the kitchen. She's in there making chili for tomorrow. Ever since she started working, she hasn't been able to cook much. She said this is one of her New Year's goals, to cook at least one recipe every week. "Hannah's here."

I toss the mouse to Butterball and walk down the stairs.

Hannah is standing in the living room with a cupcake on a paper plate. "You didn't eat this after practice. I thought maybe you'd want it now."

"Oh, thanks," I say, sitting on the couch. I'm feeling achy tonight, probably from practice. It was intense, especially the extra kicking work that Coach Missy had us do. And my throat is hurting worse. I haven't said anything about it, though, because then Mom J will rush in and stick her thermometer in my ear.

Hannah sets the cupcake on the coffee table and flops down next to me. She runs her hand through her hair and then studies her thumbnail. She seems nervous.

"Also," Hannah says after a second, "I have something to tell you."

I hold my breath and start tapping my foot fast on the wood floor.

"The thing is," Hannah says, "I'm going to stop swimming with the Dolphins. Today was my last day."

I exhale loudly. So it's true.

"I want to do volleyball," Hannah says, "and that's after school three days a week. I can't do both."

"I'll be back in a second," I say, walking to the bathroom. Partially I have to pee, but also I need to be alone for a minute. As I'm washing my hands, I stare into the mirror. What will I write on my legs at meets now? Obviously I can't write *Go Hannah Og*. And no one will be writing *Go Emme Og*, either.

When I come back, Hannah says, "Please don't be mad, Emme. We'll still be the Og Twins."

"I'm not mad," I say quietly.

Hannah smiles weakly. "Good," she says, "because we don't have to have matching swimsuits or the same haircut to be best friends. No way am I going solos on you. Get it? *Solos?*"

I try to smile at her palindrome.

Just then, Mom J walks in carrying a watering can for the plants. She brought home all these clippings from the organic garden and she's been fussing over them like they're infants.

"Emme," Mom J says, touching my forehead. "Your cheeks are bright red."

"*Redder* is another palindrome," Hannah offers. I can tell she's really trying.

Mom J sets down the watering can and comes back with the thermometer, popping it in my ear.

"One hundred and two point one," she says when it beeps. "That's a high fever, Em. Hannah, you should go before you catch it."

As soon as Hannah leaves, I lie down on the couch. Maybe Hannah is right about the swimsuits and the haircuts. And even the pizza. Maybe we don't need all those things in common. But I can't help feeling like they're part of who we are. And without them we won't be anything.

~~~~~

I have a fever for the next two days. Mom J parks me on the couch and brings me broth and tea with honey. Ms. Chung gives my homework to Jillian, who gives it to Hannah, who delivers it to Mom J at the door. One afternoon Leesa calls to check in. Mom J brings me the phone but I only stay on for five minutes. Leesa and I have talked a few times since we saw her in Connecticut, and she even said she was sorry for calling me cute, but it doesn't feel the same. I don't worship her the way I used to. Maybe that's a good thing. Maybe that's part of growing up.

On Thursday, Mom J takes me to the doctor for a throat culture. He's also Hannah's pediatrician, a tall man named Dr. Smith with a dark beard but no mustache. He reminds me of Abraham Lincoln.

"I've heard you and Hannah Strafel are best friends," Dr. Smith says as he sticks that long Q-tip down my throat.

I gag and clutch my neck. Doctors and dentists have this demented idea that you want to make casual conversation as they're ramming things in your mouth (not true).

"She's a wonderful girl," he says. "I've known Hannah since she was a toddler. I heard she's starting volleyball soon."

I nod weakly. Even my pediatrician knows that Hannah is dropping out of swimming.

That night, Hannah calls. "Are you feeling better?"

"A little," I say. "At least I don't have strep."

"And you met Dr. Abraham Lincoln."

I giggle. "I was thinking the same thing!"

"Listen," Hannah says, "I meant what I said the other day. We're still best friends even though I'm not in the Dolphins anymore."

"Okay," I say. It's one thing to hear it, though. And another (much harder) to believe it.

~~~~~

By the weekend, I'm feeling a lot better. Over breakfast on Saturday, Mom C and Mom J tell me about a winter camp called Deepwoods that Hannah's dad heard about. They even show me pictures. It's a few hours from here and takes place for three days during Presidents' Day vacation in the middle of February. I've never had a week off in February before but I guess that's a New York thing. We were supposed to visit family friends in Boston but my moms say they can shift our trip a few days earlier so we'll go before the winter camp session.

"If Hannah is going to the winter camp," I say, "then I'll go, too."

"Excellent!" Mom J says. "It sounds amazing."

As I clear the table, Mom J gets on the phone with Margo and they firm up plans. I think they all feel bad that our trip to New York City was canceled and they're hoping this will make up for it.

That afternoon, Hannah comes over to hang out.

"Can you believe we're going to Deepwoods Winter Camp?" she asks, sinking next to me on the beanbag chair.

We used to have the beanbag on our porch in Captiva, but now I keep it in my room.

"I never even knew they had winter camps," I say. "My moms said there will be sledding and tubing and ice fishing."

Not that I have any idea what ice fishing is, but it sounds fun.

"I was thinking we could decorate our bunk," Hannah said. "Like with glittery snowflakes and—"

"And pictures of pandas!" I say, squealing.

"Can you believe Sophie is coming, too?" Hannah asks.

I stare at Hannah. "Sophie?"

"Sophie," Hannah says, gesturing to the smiley face on my wall, "who used to live here. Her parents agreed to fly her down from Canada so she could join us for camp."

"Your best friend," I say quietly.

"My *other* best friend," Hannah says.

Suddenly, I start worrying all over again. What if we get to Deepwoods and Hannah and Sophie are so happy to see each other that they leave me out and—

"Emme," Hannah says, tapping my arm, "you're doing it."

"Doing what?" I ask. I have no idea what she's talking about.

"You're worrying. You've been worrying like crazy recently."

"How did you know?"

Hannah laughs. "I'm the queen of worrying. It takes one to know one. Listen. You will love Sophie. She will love you. I promise. Three is better than two."

"Are you sure?" I ask.

"Sure I'm sure."

"So what about your toenails? Have you stopped multi-color painting them?"

Hannah rolls off her socks. "Orange and yellow," she says, grinning. "I did it this morning."

I have to admit that makes me feel better.

Hannah grabs my glitter wand off my desk. She's always playing with it when she's in my room. "Let me be the worrier, okay? I worry enough for both of us."

"You'd do that for me?"

Hannah taps the wand in the center of my forehead. "Your wish is my command."

A few minutes later, I'm sketching on the floor and Hannah is flipping through some of my books. "You know how I'm supposed to pick the baby's middle name?" she asks.

"I'm thinking Levi because you can rearrange the letters and spell *evil*."

I have to laugh. "Maybe keep that brilliant idea to yourself. By the way, those letters can also spell *live*."

Hannah snorts. "I like *evil* more."

eleven

~~~~~~~~~~~~~~~~~~~~~~~~~~~~~~~~~~

HANNAH

Sophie and I have been talking on the phone a lot recently, planning for our long weekend at Deepwoods Winter Camp. She's flying in on Friday evening and my parents are driving us to the camp on Saturday. I can't believe she's taking an airplane by herself. She said that a flight attendant will be chaperoning her, but it still seems so grown up. Sophie's extra excited because she gets to miss school on Monday and Tuesday. I hadn't thought about that before, but they don't have the same Presidents' Day vacation in Canada. They also don't have Fourth of July or our Thanksgiving, either.

Two days before Sophie arrives, she tells me, "Oh, I have a pink streak in my hair now. Lots of girls in Ottawa do."

It's hard to picture Sophie with a streak in her hair. And

pink, of all colors! She's Korean and has incredibly long black hair that she's only trimmed four times in her life.

"And it's short," she says. "I got my hair cut to my shoulders with a slope from back to front."

"Really?" I ask. I pictured Sophie exactly the same as the day we said good-bye last August. "Mine is long now."

"No! I totally can't picture you with long hair."

"Yeah. I can even wear it in a ponytail."

The day before the trip, Sophie says on the phone, "I've been reading about the camp and I can't wait to try ice fishing. And everyone in Ottawa ice-skates. It sounds like you can skate to the fishing site at the camp. I might even bring my own skates."

Ugh.

For one, I wouldn't consider fishing even in the *summer*. It freaks me out to see a fish's mouth punctured with a hook, its glassy eyes staring out from either side of its head. For two, fishing AND ice-skating? No, thanks. Put me on a sled and push me down a steep hill, please. Oh, and for three, Sophie is *not* the outdoorsy type. I was surprised she said yes to Deepwoods. My dad's friend's son went and it sounds like a lot of clomping around in boots, building campfires. Sophie's more of a stay-inside-and-do-makeovers kind of girl.

I swallow hard and then ask, "You like skating now?"

I'm lying on the floor of the former guest room. When my parents aren't home I come in here and turn on the giraffe mobile and watch it wobble in circles. Usually I find it soothing. But other times I think about the baby actually arriving. Then my throat gets tight like I can't breathe and I have to leave the nursery immediately.

"Yeah, I love ice-skating now," Sophie says, laughing. "I *know*! I've become more adventuresome, if that's what you're wondering. Everyone in—"

"Everyone in Ottawa is adventuresome?" I ask.

"How did you know?"

"Lucky guess."

~~~~~

The next afternoon, my dad and I meet Sophie at the airport. Margo is tired from being a million months pregnant, so she stays home to nap. As Sophie walks through the gate, holding a pillow in one hand and a patchwork duffel bag in the other, I break into a huge smile.

"Soph!" I shout, waving and running toward her.

"Han!" she calls back to me.

We hug and then we pull back and check each other out. Something feels different about her. Her hair is short, just like she said, with a pink streak in the front. When she said *pink* she was playing it down. It's more like electric fuchsia. She's wearing eye shadow and lip gloss, which isn't new for Sophie. She's always experimented with makeup. So it's not her hair or makeup that surprises me. It's something else, something I can't put my finger on.

"I love your long hair," Sophie says. "You'd look awesome with a streak in it like mine. Maybe lime green? We could even do it tonight before—"

"Not so fast," my dad says, laughing. "I can't have you and Hannah both looking like teenagers on me."

Sophie and I roll our eyes. Okay, so maybe things will feel normal between us after all.

On the car ride back to my house, Sophie keeps pointing out the window—at the mall, the bookstore, the YMCA, Greeley Elementary.

"They're all still here!" she says over and over.

"Yep, still here," I keep answering.

My dad slows at a light and turns the radio to a music station.

"It's weird being back," Sophie says.

"Like how?"

"Like it's all familiar, but then it's not. Almost like I've never been here before. I know that sounds strange."

Of course that sounds strange! Sophie lived next door to me in Greeley for almost ten years. How can she feel like she's never been here?

Finally I ask, "How was the flight?" Boring question. But it's the best I could come up with.

"Fine," Sophie says. "You know."

"What did they give you for snacks?"

Sophie shrugs. "I think pretzels. Or maybe snack mix. I wasn't hungry."

We're quiet for a while. There's a commercial on the radio and then a song comes on. It's a pop song and, of course, Sophie knows all the words. At least that's one thing that hasn't changed.

~~~~~

On the drive up to Deepwoods the next day, I get carsick. That hasn't happened since I was five or six. But we're in the mountains and the roads are curvy and Sophie and I were flipping through a magazine. Suddenly my stomach lurches like I'm going to puke.

"Can you pull over?" I whimper to my dad. He's driving because Margo's belly is so giant she can't fit behind the steering wheel. "I'm going to be sick."

My dad steers onto the shoulder and Margo jumps out with me, holding my hair back while I hunch over the snowdrift. It's bitter cold out here. I dry heave a little, but don't actually throw up.

Once I'm back in the car, I can't stop shivering. I rest my head against the door and sip water from my bottle. Sophie offers me a piece of gum, but I don't want anything in my mouth. For a while everyone is quiet, but then Margo lets out a yelp.

"What is it?" my dad asks.

"The baby kicked, Drew," she says. "A big one."

"Are you sure it's just one baby in there, Mrs. Strafel?" Sophie asks. "Are you sure it's not twins?"

"No!" I say, lifting my head up.

"Or triplets?" Sophie asks. She grins devilishly and touches the pink streak in her hair. "Or maybe even quadruplets!"

I whimper and flop back in my seat.

"Did you forget to call me Margo?" Margo says to Sophie. "Not *Mrs. Strafel*. And yes, he's definitely just one. They do ultrasounds to figure that out."

Ultrasounds. Alien baby. Not my favorite topic.

"Speaking of twins," my dad says, "people call Hannah and Emme the *Og Twins*. Sophie, you're going to love Emme."

"Og Twins?" Sophie asks, wrinkling her nose. "What does that even mean?"

"Nothing," I say, shaking my head. I don't feel like getting into the whole story about how we used to write on our legs at swim meets. I'm worried if I talk too much I'll have to puke. "It's hard to explain."

"Am I going to like Emme?" Sophie asks me. "I feel jealous that she lives in my house."

Emme and her moms were visiting friends in Boston for the past few days, so she and Sophie haven't met each other yet. Emme's moms are dropping her off at Deepwoods on their way back to Greeley. She might even be at the camp already.

"Emme is wonderful," my dad says.

"And don't start the jealousy thing," Margo says. "You girls will all get along great."

Sophie shrugs like she's not so sure. I close my eyes. Maybe this wasn't such a good idea after all.

~~~~~

Our cabin is called Icicles. That's what our counselor, Meredith, tells us as Sophie and I trek across a path packed with snow. Deepwoods is in a valley, so it's not as freezing cold as up on the main road. Meredith is probably twenty and has glasses and a hat with earflaps. Sophie and I are wearing our backpacks. Our suitcases will be delivered on a pickup truck later. Even though we'll only be here for three days, we had to bring a ton of winter gear, like boots and snow pants and long underwear.

"In the summer camp season, we call the cabin Sunflower," Meredith says as she points to the lodge and the camp store and the sledding hill. "But we change the names in the winter. Icicles is for fifth-grade girls. We also have Snowball and Blizzard. That's a boys' cabin."

Sophie grins at me and raises her eyebrows. *Huh?* Does she like boys now? It's strange how I can't read her expressions anymore.

When we get into Icicles, Meredith pulls off her hat and shakes out her long curly hair. She shows us where we hang our coats and snow pants, and the rack near the heater where we'll dry our boots at night.

"But don't take off your boots now," she says. "We're going to head up to the main lodge in a few minutes for hot chocolate in front of the fireplace. That's where we'll have the welcome ceremony."

"Is Emme Hoffman-Shields here yet?" I ask.

"She has a hyphenated name?" Sophie asks. She's holding her pillow under one arm. For some reason, she insisted on bringing it all the way from Canada even though the camp said they'd be providing pillows.

"She hasn't arrived yet," Meredith says, checking her list. "But speaking of Emme"—she turns to Sophie—"you two have been assigned to share a bunk bed. You can decide now whether you want the top or bottom bunk, or you can wait until she arrives."

My stomach flips. *Oh, no.* Please not the pukey feeling again.

"What about me?" I ask. I thought *I'd* be in a bunk bed with one of them. After all, they're *my* best friends.

"The number of campers wasn't even this year," Meredith says, "so you'll actually have a bed to yourself." She smiles brightly in the way people do when they're delivering bad news that they're trying to package as good news. "That means you don't have to battle it out for top or bottom bunk."

Meredith gestures to a lumpy-looking single bed off to one side of the cabin, way far away from the bunk beds, next to the doorway leading to the bathroom.

"Single bed," Sophie says. "Lucky."

But she says it in this way that she's *really* thinking I didn't get so lucky.

~~~~~~

A few minutes later, Emme walks into the door of Icicles with a pillow under her arm. She brought a pillow, too? The next thing I notice is that Emme has a streak of blue in her hair, just in front of her left ear. She got a streak in her hair, too? We haven't talked in a few days since she's been in Boston. I hadn't even told her about Sophie's pink streak.

"Surprise!" Emme says to me. "I had my streak done at a salon yesterday. What do you think?"

"Nice," I say, shrugging. I glance over at Sophie. "This is Emme," I say. Then I turn to Emme and say, "This is Sophie."

Emme notices the pink streak in Sophie's hair and Sophie notices the blue streak in Emme's hair and they both start laughing.

"I love your hair!" Emme says to Sophie. "Hannah didn't say you had pink in it."

I thought Emme hated pink.

"We hadn't talked," I say.

"I love your hair, too! You have such a cute bob and I love the blue," Sophie says to Emme. "You went to a salon for it? Lucky! I had to do mine at home. And I love that you're living in my old bedroom."

I thought Sophie was jealous of Emme taking over her house.

"I've heard *everything* about you," Emme says to Sophie. "Did you hear I kept your smiley face on my bedroom wall?"

Sophie squeals. "Really? That's so cool! Why didn't you tell me, Hannah?"

"You didn't ask," I say.

"Did you know we're sharing a bunk bed?" Sophie asks Emme.

"Do you care whether you're on the bottom or top bunk?" Emme asks.

"Not really," Sophie says.

"Me neither!" Emme says.

They both giggle and then they hug. They HUG. My two best friends have known each other for thirty-seven seconds and they're *hugging*.

As Emme and Sophie arrange their pillows on their beds, I sit on the edge of my misshapen mattress. It turns out my bed is also right under the sloped roof. If I'm not careful when I sit up, I'll bonk my head.

"Five minutes until the welcome ceremony," Meredith says. A bunch of other girls have trickled into the bunk and she's showing them around.

I glance over at Emme and Sophie's bunk bed area and I'm shocked to see them both taping up pictures of pandas on the wall. They *both* brought pictures of *pandas*?

I push myself off the bed and walk over to them. "You like pandas now?" I ask Sophie.

"Who doesn't?" she says.

Maybe me, I think darkly. Maybe I'll be the only person in the world who hates the panda bear.

~~~~~

On the way to the welcome ceremony, I pause to cinch the elastic on the top of my boot. When I catch up, Emme and Sophie have linked elbows. They're singing a song about being made out of glue and sticking together.

"What are you singing?" I ask.

"Just something I heard on the drive from Boston," Emme says. "Want me to teach you?"

I shake my head. I consider reminding her of the song

"Make New Friends (But Keep the Old)." Instead I stoop over and cinch my other boot tighter.

At dinner, I sit across from Emme and Sophie. They don't stop talking the entire time. It's like they're long-lost best friends. When the director stands up to make a speech, they both whistle instead of clap. At the evening sing-along after dinner, they get the other kids going in a round of "Row, Row, Row Your Boat." Forget about long-lost friends. They're the exact same person!

"What's with the killer stare?" Sophie says as we're walking over to the tables to sign up for tomorrow's activities. For once, she and Emme aren't stuck together like glue.

"What killer stare?" I ask innocently. So maybe I was glaring a little, but I thought she was too busy bonding with Emme to notice.

Sophie rolls her eyes like *whatever* and then grabs a pen and starts reading the sign-up sheets.

"Oooh, look," Sophie says. "They have ice-skating tomorrow morning!"

I've had enough. I squeeze through the crowd, zip up my coat, and walk to the camp store. Meredith told us that's where they sell things like spare toothpaste and Deepwoods key chains and sweatshirts. They also have a computer you can use to email your parents. I sit on the hard wooden bench, log onto my email, and write to my dad and Margo.

> Hey,
> I don't think I like it here. I'm sorry, but it's true.
> Hannah

I send the email and then head slowly back to the lodge. On the way, I hit my forehead on a low pine branch. An avalanche of snow pours down the back of my coat.

I might actually hate this place.

~~~~~

At seven thirty the next morning, a bugle plays "Reveille" over the camp loudspeaker. I sit up too quickly and whack the top of my head on the ceiling. Two head injuries in less than twelve hours. Nice.

I glance across the cabin. Most girls are rubbing their eyes and pushing their hair out of their faces. But Emme and Sophie's bunk bed is empty.

The toilet flushes, rattling the water bottle on the shelf next to my bed.

"Where are Emme and Sophie?" I ask Meredith as she steps out of the bathroom.

"Polar bear ice-skating," she says, twisting her curls into a loose bun. "They signed up for it last night after dinner. They're having a picnic breakfast on the lake."

They've ice-skated onto the lake to eat *breakfast*? I can't believe this winter camp was *my* parents' idea. I should have said no right away!

Meredith must see the look on my face because she says, "Don't worry. I noticed that you didn't sign up for a morning activity yet. After breakfast, we can get you fitted in skates and you can join them for ice fishing. What happened to your forehead? You have a red mark."

"Nothing." I touch my head with my fingers. "I'm fine."

Meredith leans in closer and peers at my forehead. I try to keep my mouth from quivering. I suddenly feel like I'm going to cry.

At breakfast, I sit with the other girls from my bunk, but I barely say anything. My toast is dry and the eggs taste like rubber. I wonder what Sophie and Emme are eating out there with the other polar bears.

For my morning activity, I sign up for arts and crafts. It's

just me and two other girls in a musty cabin, gluing together
Popsicle sticks to make birdhouses. None of my Popsicle sticks
line up and I forget to make a door or windows. My birdhouse
ends up looking like a lopsided jail.

~~~~~

I run into Emme on the front porch of the dining hall. It's a
few minutes before lunch. I was sitting on a bench trying to
adjust my left boot. For some reason, it's either too tight or too
loose. Emme plops down next to me. Her cheeks are bright
red and her pale blue scarf is wrapped around the lower half
of her face.

"How's it going?" she asks. "We missed you on the ice this
morning. It was amazing. I can't believe I skated on a real lake!"

"Good for you," I say. I don't look up from my boot.

"Too bad I hid a boot," Emme says.

When I don't respond, she says, "Palindrome alert. Did
you know that one?"

When I still don't respond, she says, "What's wrong,
Hannah? Are you mad we went ice-skating without you?"

I shrug. I have that feeling like I'm going to cry again.
"Where's your best friend?"

Emme touches her gloves together, lining up her fingers one by one. "What's that supposed to mean?" she asks quietly. "You know you're my best friend."

I stare hard at her. "I do?"

Emme looks away. "If you're wondering where Sophie is, she went to reserve tubes for the sledding hill this afternoon. We heard that the good ones go first."

"How nice."

"She's getting three tubes. For the three of us." Emme holds up three gloved fingers. "I told her to get a blue tube for you."

I clench my teeth. All I want right now is to be back in Greeley, in my house, in my room.

"You could at least say thanks," Emme says.

She's asking me to *thank* her? This is too much. WAY too much.

"Thanks a lot," I say sarcastically.

"You know," Emme says, "you're being really awful. Sophie thinks so, too. I'm sorry we went skating without you but I didn't think—"

"Didn't think what?" I snap. "Didn't think I'd care that my two best friends like each other more than they like me?"

Emme pushes her scarf down so it's around her neck. "I thought you *wanted* us to get along."

The lunch bell clangs and a bunch of people wander onto the porch. I wait until they're inside the dining hall and then I say, "I don't know what I want."

Emme presses her lips together. I don't think I've ever seen her look this angry. "It's not a hard question, Hannah. Do you want me to get along with Sophie or not?"

"I don't know if Sophie is who she was before," I say to Emme. "I think she's changed."

"Maybe you've changed!" Emme shouts, pointing her finger in my face. "You eat pizza now and you dropped out of swimming and your mom is having a baby."

"Like that's my fault!" I scream, so loudly that people coming up the path stare at us.

"I'm just saying that I'm dealing with your changes and—"

"I didn't know you had to DEAL with me," I say, jumping to my feet.

"Listen." Emme pushes off the bench, too. "I'm sorry we went ice-skating without you this morning, but it was actually nice not having you sulk the whole time. Deal with that. I have to pee."

Emme stomps through the door of the dining hall. As I

watch her go, I suddenly have that feeling like I can't breathe. It's similar to what I've had before, when I was in the baby's room, but much worse. I run back to the bunk. When I get inside, I clutch my hands to my throat and keel forward, trying to suck in air.

After a while, my counselor pushes open the door to Icicles.

"Hannah?" Meredith asks, sitting next to me on the bed. "I heard you were upset. Are you okay?"

I shake my head. The tears are coming, but I don't care. Because everything is hitting me at once. Sophie and me growing apart. Sophie and Emme getting along so well. Emme saying she was glad I wasn't polar bear ice-skating with them. The new baby. Getting adopted.

"Can you tell me what's going on?" Meredith asks. She takes off her glasses. "You came with Sophie Park, right? Want me to have someone get her?"

I shake my head. Everything feels mixed up right now, like my whole life is changing and there's nothing I can do to stop any of it. "I just . . . I want to go home."

"A lot of people feel that way on the first day of camp. I can take you over to the infirmary. The nurse can check out that mark on your forehead and maybe she'll—"

"No," I say, shaking my head. "Can you please call my parents? I want them to pick me up. I want to go home."

This time it sinks in with Meredith. She knows I'm not kidding. I want this to be over. Emme's mom Julia was planning to drive us all back to Greeley after camp. Now she can just get Emme and Sophie. They'll probably be happier without me anyway.

Meredith goes into the bathroom and comes back with a few sheets of toilet paper for me to blow my nose. Once I've dried my face, I pack my suitcase and backpack and grab my snow pants off the peg. On the way out of Icicles, I tape a note to the side of Emme and Sophie's bunk bed.

Enjoy each other

—Hannah

And then I walk out.

twelve

~~~~~~~~~~~~~~~~~~~~~~

EMME

Hannah and I haven't talked in three and a half days, not since our fight outside the dining hall. Part of that time, I was at Deepwoods. Try having fun at camp after your best friend has ditched you without saying good-bye (and might not even be your best friend anymore).

For the past day and a half, I've been back home. It's still February break and I'm right here, right next door to Hannah. I've seen her hanging a Popsicle-stick birdhouse on their side porch with Margo and playing basketball in her driveway with her uncle. One time, when Mom J and I were getting in the car to go to the mall for new clothes (yes, I finally grew a full inch), Hannah and her dad were getting *out* of their car with bags from the Gap and Old Navy. Our parents said hi, but we didn't look at each other.

I'm so mad that Hannah ran away from camp like that. Yes, maybe Sophie and I should have told her we signed up for polar bear ice-skating. But Hannah was moody from the second I arrived. Plus, it's obvious she hates ice-skating. I knew she wouldn't want to come. And that note she wrote! *Enjoy each other.* That made Sophie and me cry.

After Hannah left Deepwoods, I only skated one more time. Sophie and I tried to have fun together, but it was awkward. Sophie was stressed because she was going back to Hannah's house and sleeping over before she flew home to Canada. I was upset because maybe it's true that the Og Twins are over.

But it's not all my fault!

I'm sick of the way Hannah has a meltdown whenever things don't go her way, like when the New York City trip was canceled or when Sophie and I realized we actually got along. (It turns out Sophie was as nervous about meeting me as I was about meeting her.)

The thing is, even with everything that's happened, I really miss Hannah. I just want this fight to be over. I start crying whenever I think about it.

Mom J and Margo had a long talk yesterday, to see if they could help. According to Margo, Hannah still needs time to cool off. I know what *that* means. It's a gentle way of saying she wants nothing to do with me. And the truth is, if Hannah and I were in the same room, I don't know what I'd say to her either.

I took down the first-place ribbon that Hannah made for me and put it in my dresser. It hurt too much to look at it.

Even the blue streak in my hair isn't making me happy.

I am definitely in a doom mood.

～～～

On Thursday morning, Mom C is at work and Mom J is at the greenhouse. They're having kindergarten camp this week, and Mom J has been volunteering at it. She invited me to come along today, but when I considered choice one (herding five-years-olds wielding spades through a room of dirt) versus choice two (sketching, reading, snacking, screen time), it was a no-brainer.

Around ten, I'm walking to the fridge for a glass of orange juice when I notice Butterball's dish is full of food.

Oh, no. Not again.

Sure, it's his (even grosser) diet food, but he wolfs it down in eight seconds anyway.

I quickly check the shelf for his yellow collar. Phew. At least he has his cat tags on. But why didn't he eat breakfast?

Did he run away again? What if he ran to Hannah's house like before and when I go get him she tells me to my face that she never wants to be friends again?

Just then, I hear a whimper coming from the downstairs bathroom. It's like a meow but it sounds weak and muffled. I run into the bathroom and there's Butterball, sprawled on the floor under the sink. His eyes are half closed and his body looks limp. I try to rouse him, but he won't move.

I hurry to the phone and dial Mom J.

"Emme?" she asks, answering on the second ring. "Is everything okay?"

"It's Butterball," I manage to say. "He's collapsed. I'm not sure he's even . . ." I can't say *alive* out loud. Butterball has been my cat since I was six. There's no way he can die on me.

"I'll be right home," she says. "Get the travel case ready. I'll call Dr. Konning and tell her we're on our way."

I'm trying to hold it together, but the tears are coming. "What should I do with Butterball until you get here?"

"Just hold him," Mom J says. "Sit with him. I'm sure he'll feel better knowing you're there."

As soon as Mom J hangs up, I stand at the door of the bathroom. I'm shaking all over. What if Butterball *is* dead? But no. His chest is slowly rising and falling. He's breathing.

Even so, I'm scared to be alone with him. After I get the travel case out of the hall closet, I go to the phone and call Hannah.

"Hello?" a man's voice asks. It doesn't sound like her dad.

"Hey, this is Emme."

"Hi! This is Uncle Peter. Let me get Hannah."

I hear talking in the background. *Please come to the phone,* I silently will Hannah. *Please, please, please.*

"Hey," she says after a second.

As soon as I hear her voice, I start crying all over again. "It's Butterball. Something really bad has happened to him. He's barely conscious."

"Are you serious?" Hannah asks. "When?"

"Right now. My mom is on her way home. We're taking him to the vet."

"I'll be right over," she says.

Three seconds later, Hannah bangs at our front door and I let her in. She's in slippers and she's not even wearing a coat. We hurry into the bathroom.

I can barely look at Butterball, but Hannah slides her hands under him and lifts him into her lap. She pets him and whispers "It's okay" over and over again. I notice he looks a lot skinnier now, and his fur is droopy and loose.

"Hannah?" I say, sitting so close to her that our knees are touching. I have the hugest lump in my throat. "I'm sorry about the things I said at camp and how Sophie and I left you out. I didn't mean I had to *deal* with you. I just meant—"

"I know you didn't," Hannah says. "I *was* being awful. You were right when you said that. It wasn't fair the way I took it out on you. I've been upset about the baby coming and it was weird seeing Sophie again. But that wasn't your fault. I've been wanting to say I'm sorry to you but . . ." Hannah pauses.

We're both wiping tears from our eyes and gently stroking Butterball's back.

"What?" I ask.

"I was worried if I talked to you, you'd say you didn't want to be best friends anymore," Hannah says.

"Of course not. I'd never say that."

"So we're still the Og Twins?" Hannah asks.

"Always."

At the exact same time, we reach over and hug each other. I'm careful not to press into Butterball or hurt him in any way.

"The thing is," Hannah says after a second, "there's something else going on, too."

"What?"

"Margo went into labor. She left for the hospital an hour ago. That's why my uncle—"

"Your mom is having the baby *right now*?" I ask, my voice rising.

Hannah nods slowly.

We sit in stunned silence until we hear Mom J's car pull into the driveway.

thirteen

~~~~~~~~~~~

HANNAH

This whole morning, it feels like everything has been going really fast. Or really slow. Or maybe both.

Ever since I came downstairs for breakfast, Margo was having contractions and my dad was timing them and talking on the phone to the obstetrician. I kept telling them they should GO TO THE HOSPITAL! But they said they had to wait until the contractions were five minutes apart for an entire hour. Which seems bizarre. The last thing we want is for the alien baby to come out in our living room. That's the part that was going slow.

But then they declared it was time to GO TO THE HOSPITAL! and it became a hurricane. Uncle Peter burst in the door and grabbed the suitcase and my dad helped Margo into the car. Thirty seconds later, my parents peeled down the driveway. That was definitely fast.

Then time got really slow again. Uncle Peter and I sat at the kitchen table, eating salted almonds and watching the clock. Our conversation went something like this:

Uncle Peter: Are you okay?

Me: Yeah, are you?

Uncle Peter: Fine. Do you think they're at the hospital yet?

Me: Maybe. Probably not.

Uncle Peter: You sure you're okay?

Me: I guess so. Do you think they're at the hospital now?

Uncle Peter: Maybe. Probably. Want more almonds?

But then Emme called. I was SO relieved when Uncle Peter said it was her. I feel terrible about Deepwoods. I can't believe I took off without even telling her or Sophie. I was sure Emme didn't want to be friends after that. Margo kept saying that forgiveness is part of friendship, but I had no idea how I'd ask Emme to forgive me.

It was easier to make up with Sophie. When she got back to my house after camp, Margo let her in the front door and she and I were just like "Hey, what's up?" I said I was sorry and Sophie said it was okay. She didn't say anything about Emme and I didn't ask. We ordered pizza and watched a movie, and my dad and I drove her to the airport early the next morning.

But it felt different with Emme. Maybe because we'd actually yelled at each other. Also, I think it's because Emme and I have gotten so close this year, and Sophie and I have grown apart. I've been thinking a lot about friendship these past few days. I've been thinking how there are different kinds of friendship, and how friendships can even change over time. Like, Sophie will always be a certain kind of friend because I've known her my whole life. But Emme is my in-every-way best friend, the person I want to see every single day and tell everything to.

When Uncle Peter handed me the phone, Emme told me that Butterball was sick. That's when things got fast again. I ran over and stayed with Emme until Julia arrived. Then I sprinted back to my house for my coat and sneakers and to tell Uncle Peter where I was going. Julia and Emme put Butterball in the backseat. Now we're driving to the vet. Butterball is in his case, between Emme and me. He's lying completely still with his eyes closed. I've never seen a sick cat before, but I have to say he doesn't look good. Not that I'm going to tell Emme. Not that I have to.

"He doesn't look good," Emme says to her mom. "Do you think he's going to make it?"

"Dr. Konning is the best vet around," Julia says. "If anyone can help Butterball, she can."

We pull into the parking lot of the brick building. As soon as Emme slides out, Julia gets the cat case from the back and we all hurry into the vet's office.

"I'm Julia Hoffman," Emme's mom says to the woman sitting at the front desk. "I called a few minutes ago about our cat, Butterball. It's an emergency."

"Oh, yes," the receptionist says, picking up her phone. "Dr. Morris is ready for you. I'll let him know you're here."

"Dr. *Morris?*" Emme asks her mom. Her voice sounds high and tight.

Julia shrugs. "They just said to come in immediately. They didn't say anything about—"

"Dr. Konning isn't in today," the receptionist says. "Dr. Morris is her partner."

Emme pulls on her mom's sleeve. "But you said—"

A tall man in a lab coat opens the door to an examination room. He smiles and holds out his hand to Emme's mom. He has balding orange hair and extremely large front teeth.

As soon as we get inside the brightly lit room, he scoops Butterball into his arms and says, "What have we got here? Not feeling so good?"

He starts by listening to Butterball's pulse and taking his blood pressure. Dr. Morris is working quickly, but he doesn't look panicked.

"His blood pressure is low," he tells us, "but that doesn't surprise me."

Emme whimpers and covers her eyes.

"We're going to run blood work," Dr. Morris says. "We'll have the preliminary results in an hour."

As the vet goes to the counter for a needle, Emme moans, "I don't feel so good."

Julia whips her head around. "What is it, Em?"

"I just . . ." Emme looks pale as she sinks back in her chair. "I don't want to see him get a shot."

"Want to go out to the waiting room with me?" I ask.

Emme nods and I help her up. Her hand feels cold.

"Thanks, Hannah," Julia says. "I know you've got a lot on your mind, too. I texted your dad and told him to keep us posted."

I try to smile, but it probably looks more like a grimace. I'd honestly like to imagine that Margo is at work and my dad is at work and today is a regular day.

"I'll take good care of your cat," Dr. Morris reassures Emme as we walk out of the room.

"Thanks," she says weakly.

Emme and I first stop by the water cooler at the end of the hallway. I had no idea my mouth was so dry. I'm feeling better after downing two cups of water, and Emme looks slightly steadier, too.

But then we walk into the waiting room and there, sitting on the couch, is Alexa Morris playing on an iPad. She's all by herself, no parent or pet in sight.

Great. Just great. Alexa was one of the girls in Ms. Linhart's class who was mean to Emme. Gina was the worst, but Alexa wasn't much better. Who knows? Maybe she was even the one who wrote *LOSER* on Emme's collage.

I glance at Emme. I expect her to drop her water cup or turn away, but she stares right at Alexa and says, "Why're you here?"

Alexa is so surprised that her mouth hangs open. She twists a rubber band on her wrist and says, "Uh, my dad is the vet. Dr. Morris."

Duh. Of course. Dr. *Morris*. Alexa *Morris*. Red hair. Big teeth.

"My cat is really sick," Emme says, sitting on a chair across from Alexa. "Your dad is in there with him."

"That's good," Alexa says. "He's really good."

I sit next to Emme. None of us say anything. I wonder what Emme is thinking. She doesn't seem shy like she used to whenever Alexa and her crew sat near us in the cafeteria.

"You were awful last fall," Emme suddenly says to Alexa. "You made moving here really hard for me."

I don't know who is more shocked, me or Alexa. I'm staring at Emme, completely in awe. Alexa is staring at the ground like she's going to cry.

"It's not like I want you to say sorry," Emme says. "I'm just saying you should think about how you treat people. And people's stuff, too. I liked that collage. I was making it with my cousin."

Alexa's eyes are bloodshot and she's wiping at her nose. She reaches for a tissue, but then shreds it in her hands. "I'm not friends with Gina anymore if that's what you're wondering," she whispers. "Neither is Haley."

Emme nods. I stare at the clock on the wall. Time is slowing down again.

"I hope your cat is okay," Alexa says.

"Me too," Emme says.

"He will be," I say, squeezing Emme's hand. "I know he will be."

I'm not usually such an optimist, but I'm going to act like one until Emme's ready to be one again.

~~~~~~

It turns out Butterball has diabetes. Emme thought he was losing weight because of the diet cat food and his new exercise routine, but he was actually getting sick all along. Dr. Morris told us that he had something called ketoacidosis, which is a medical way of saying his body was starting to shut down. Luckily we got him to the vet quickly, and Dr. Morris thinks he's going to pull through.

The bad news is that he'll have to stay at the vet's office for the next few days, receiving medicine through a tube they put in his paw. They have rooms in the back. They keep the dogs in a separate room so the other animals aren't traumatized by barking. When we went to say good-bye, Butterball was in a cage right next to a cat who'd had surgery, and above an iguana with a broken arm. Butterball had tape around his paw where the tube was going in, but he didn't seem to mind. He nuzzled his nose into my hand, and Emme thought she heard him purring.

The good news is that diabetes is treatable. I told Emme how Margo's dad, my Pop-Pop, has diabetes. He just has to be careful about what he eats, and give himself insulin injections every day. When Emme heard that, she practically passed out, but Julia assured her that she wouldn't be the one giving Butterball his shots.

I'm sleeping over at Emme's house tonight. Uncle Peter said it's okay. The crazy thing is, Margo hasn't had the baby yet even though she's been at the hospital for nine hours. Julia talked to my dad and he said everything is fine, that some babies take longer to come out than others. Even though they're all reassuring me that it's okay, I'm so worried about Margo. She just officially became my mom. I don't want anything to happen to her.

Claire makes us stir-fry for dinner and we watch some shows. Around nine thirty, I roll out a sleeping bag on Emme's floor and Emme climbs into her bed.

This feels like it's been the longest day of my entire life.

As I'm adjusting my pillow, I think about how many times I slept in this room back when Sophie used to live here. That makes me think about what happened at Deepwoods. I'm so glad Emme and I made up.

Emme turns out the light. I'm just starting to fall asleep when she says, "Are you excited about the baby coming?"

When she says that, my heart flutters nervously. I'm about

to say, *Sure, whatever,* but then I decide to tell her the truth. There's something about being in the dark that makes it feel okay to open up.

"Ever since I heard that my parents were having a baby," I say, "I've been dreading it. And now it's finally happening."

"Is that why you didn't tell me about it for so long?"

"I guess so." I pause for a second. "I actually found out that Margo was pregnant, like, five minutes before you moved in. I was on the side porch to get away from them when you guys pulled up."

"That explains a lot," Emme says.

"Yeah," I say.

"Want to hear the funny thing? I would love a little brother. Sometimes being an only child, it feels like my moms are watching me all the time. Like, I wish they were distracted with another kid."

"You can have him," I mutter.

When Emme doesn't say anything, I take a deep breath. "I'm also a little excited. I'm just worried they'll love him more than they love me. Maybe that sounds stupid, but it's true. Also, I don't want to have to deal with dirty diapers and crying and the baby spitting up milk all over the place."

I can hear Emme rolling over in her bed. "I have an idea."

"What?"

"When the baby gets to be too much, you come over here. This can be your place to escape. A baby-free zone."

I nod in the dark. A baby-free zone sounds nice.

"Also," Emme says, "remember how we agreed to share Butterball last fall, and you said you'd help me take care of him?"

"Yeah." Thinking about Butterball makes my stomach flip over. I can't believe he and Margo are *both* in the hospital right now.

"I can help you take care of the baby," Emme says. "I can be like a bonus big sister to him. We can teach him things and deal with gross spit-up together and when your parents are getting annoying with the baby love, we can tell them to chillax with taking photos every two seconds."

"Chillax?" I ask.

Emme laughs. "Chill. Relax."

"Is that something your cousin Leesa says?"

"Nope," she says. "It's an Emme original."

After a few minutes, I hear Emme's steady breathing. I thought it was going to take forever to fall asleep, but I close my eyes and I'm out in four seconds.

~~~

In the morning, Claire knocks on the door. She told us last night that she was going to take a vacation day from work today.

"Do you want baby news or cat news?" she asks, walking to the window and opening the curtain. It's gray out, but still bright.

Emme sits up in bed and rubs her eyes. "Baby news."

"Yeah, baby news," I say, wriggling out of my sleeping bag. After Emme and my talk last night, I'm feeling better about this new baby.

Claire grins and holds out her phone. "Your dad is waiting for your call."

I take the phone and stare down at it.

"Do you want privacy?" Claire asks. "Emme and I can step out for a minute."

"No, that's okay. Actually, please stay in here."

As the phone is ringing, I can barely breathe. But it's not like before, when I was upset. This time it's because I'm excited.

"Claire?" my dad says into the phone. "Is Hannah awake?"

"It's me, Dad," I say. As soon as I hear his voice, I can't stop smiling.

"Hey, honey!" my dad says. "Margo had the baby around midnight. He's healthy and they're both doing great. I'd put Margo on except she's sleeping."

"What's his name?" Emme whispers, tugging on my hand.

"Shhh," Claire says.

"What's his name?" I ask my dad.

"Thank you," Emme says, falling back on her bed.

"Spencer," my dad says. "Spencer Strafel. All he needs now is a middle name."

"Spencer," I tell Emme.

"So cute!" she says, sitting up again.

"Shhh," Claire says. "Seriously."

"What does he look like?" I ask.

My dad groans and says, "To us, he's adorable. He barely has any hair. Honestly, he looks a little like an alien. I guess you predicted that one."

I have to laugh.

"As soon as we hang up, I'll text a picture to Claire's phone."

"Okay," I say. "Good-bye!"

"Hannah?" my dad asks. "I love you. I'll see you later this morning, okay?"

"I love you, too. Now good-bye. Send a picture."

We hang up and a second later a text appears on Claire's phone.

"Can I look at it?" I ask.

"Of course!" Claire says.

Emme scrambles over and we both study the screen.

"He's so small," Emme coos.

"Not that small," Claire says. "He was eight and a half pounds."

I look at the picture of Spencer's face. He's wearing a striped hat pulled low over his forehead. Actually he doesn't look at all like an alien. He has a tiny baby nose and pink lips and his eyes are open. His expression looks confused, like *who am I and what am I doing here?* It makes me want to give him a kiss and tell him everything will be okay.

"Congratulations on becoming a sister, Hannah," Emme says.

I'm about to say *former only child*, but instead I just say, "Thanks."

They're both staring at me and grinning, so I say, "What about cat news?"

"Yeah, how's Butterball?" Emme asks.

"So much better," Claire says. "We just talked to Dr.

Morris and he went in early to check on him. His vitals are good and he's even drinking water. He's going to be okay. We can visit him anytime this morning."

Emme exhales slowly. I snuggle back into my sleeping bag.

Once Claire leaves, Emme asks, "What if we made a mistake and brought catnip to your brother and a rattle to Butterball?"

"Or diapers to Butterball!" I say.

"And a collar with a little bell for Spencer!" Emme says.

I start laughing, and Emme laughs along with me. Pretty soon, we're laughing so hard our eyes are watering and we're rolling around on her bedroom floor.

fourteen

~~~~~~~~~~~~

EMME

"People hospital or animal hospital first?" Mom J says at breakfast.

"People hospital!" Hannah and I shout at the same time.

Mom C made us a huge breakfast. Blueberry pancakes, sausages, grapefruit cut in half, even some of the applesauce that Mom J and I canned in the fall. Hannah and I both have our plates piled high. We picked at the stir-fry last night and didn't even have dessert, so we're crazy hungry now.

Hannah's uncle had to go to work this morning, so Mom J and Mom C are driving Hannah to the hospital. My moms said they could arrange for Hannah's dad to meet her in the lobby and bring her up to see Margo and Spencer, in case she wanted family time, but she said she wanted me to come with her. We're in this together, after all. I'm so excited about being a bonus sister. Plus, I've never seen a nine-hour-old baby before!

Once we're done eating, we clear our plates and then Mom J comes out of the bathroom with her downstairs thermometer (yes, she has now purchased one to keep upstairs as well).

"What's that for?" I ask, dodging her as she's coming toward my ear.

"I want to make sure you're both healthy," she says. "Newborns are very susceptible to colds."

"Good idea," Hannah says. "We also have to wash our hands a lot."

As Hannah offers her ear to Mom J, I realize how much she sounds like a big sister all of a sudden.

We're both fever-free (as if I didn't know that) so I go up to my room to get dressed and Hannah runs to her house for fresh clothes. My moms recently told me that we're going to Captiva Island for spring break to visit friends, but Greeley is actually feeling like my home now. I pull on a pair of jeans and the long-sleeve orange shirt that Mom J got me at the Gap and then glance in the mirror. I love the blue streak in my hair. I can't wait to go back to school on Monday and see what people say about it.

When I get downstairs, Hannah is in the kitchen. She's wearing the exact same long-sleeve orange shirt that I am.

"No way!" I say. "No. Way."

Hannah looks over at me. "No way! When did you get it?"

"Wednesday," I say. "At the mall."

"Me too!" she says.

We both crack up. What a totally Og Twins occurrence. It reminds me of that first day we met, how we both had on the same tie-dye tank top. I actually tried mine on recently and it was too small.

On the way to the hospital, Hannah is chewing her nails and tapping one foot against the car floor. That's what she does when she's nervous. I keep trying to distract her, but it's not working.

"I've got a good palindrome," I say. *"As I pee, sir, I see Pisa."*

"Thanks a lot," Hannah says, groaning. "That just made me want to pee."

"Now you're turning into me!"

We pull into the circular driveway in front of Greeley Memorial Hospital. My moms drop us off, and then they drive to a deli to get sandwiches for Hannah's parents.

We step into the elevator and Hannah pushes 10. Mom C told us that that's the baby floor.

On the ride up, I say to Hannah, "Have you decided?"

Hannah knows exactly what I'm taking about. "The way I see it," she says, "there are three or four palindrome boys' names. There's Bob, of course."

"But that doesn't sound like a baby," I say. "That sounds like a fifty-year-old fisherman."

Hannah nods. We're now passing the third floor. We have seven more floors to decide.

"What about Izzi?" Hannah asks. "Or Natan."

"Pretty good," I say. Now fifth floor. Now sixth floor. I know Hannah wants to have this figured out before she sees Spencer. "What about Otto?"

"Otto," Hannah says. "Spencer Otto Strafel."

We're just coming up to nine. "His initials would be S.O.S."

"Which is cool," Hannah says.

"And *also* happens to be a palindrome," I add.

The elevator dings at ten.

"That's perfect," Hannah says as the doors open.

We step off the elevator and walk down the hall, arm in arm, to meet Hannah's little brother and give him his middle name.

acknowledgments

A huge thanks to my kid advisory crew: Miles Rideout, Equem Roël, Remy Roël, and Laura Jayne Grant.

Thanks to the adults, too: Jonas Rideout, David Levithan, Jodi Reamer, Anne Dalton, Kelly O'Neill Levy, Deb Grant, Melanie Levy Fagelson, Maxine Roël, Myrna Gunning, Barbara Stretchberry, Kristi Thom, and Adriane Frye.

Thanks to The JCC in Manhattan for letting me watch swim team practice.

Thanks to Stephanie Rath, the original best friend next door.

And a special thanks to Leif Rideout, who really wanted me to write a book about pandas.

riendship. Fun. First crushes.

11 Birthdays

WENDY MASS

sit,
stay,
love

J.J. Howard

cake
pop
crush

suzanne nelson

My Secret Guide to Paris

LISA SCHROEDER

12
Finally

WENDY MASS

REVENGE OF THE FLOWER GIRLS

They will stop at nothing to stop this wedding

JENNIFER ZIEGLER

macarons at midnight

the BOY project

a novel by KAMI KINARD

Switched at Birthday

Natalie Standiford

ONCE UPON A CRUISE

wish

SCHOLASTIC™ Scholastic Inc.

scholastic.com/wish

WISH20SPREAD

Read all the WISH books!

To learn more about the 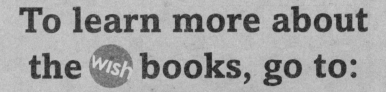 books, go to:

scholastic.com/wish